Trusting My Heart
with the
King of New York

Trusting My Heart with the King of New York

Desia'Ra

www.urbanbooks.net

Urban Books, LLC
300 Farmingdale Road, N.Y.-Route 109
Farmingdale, NY 11735

ISBN 13: 978-1-64556-701-1

First Trade Paperback Printing May 2025
Printed in the United States of America

10 9 8 7 6 5 4 3 2 1

Distributed by Kensington Publishing Corp.
Submit Orders to:
Customer Service
400 Hahn Road
Westminster, MD 21157-4627
Phone: 1-800-733-3000
Fax: 1-800-659-2436

The authorized representative in the EU for product safety and compliance
Is eucomply OU, Parnu mnt 139b-14, Apt 123
Tallinn, Berlin 11317, hello@eucompliancepartner.com

Trusting My Heart with the King of New York

Desia'Ra

Acknowledgments

and Dedication

I would like to dedicate this book to my baby girl, Laya. Baby girl, I love you more than words can ever say. These past few years that I have been blessed to be your mother have been amazing. You are the one who makes me strive to be better than I was yesterday. I am completely honored that God chose me to be your mother, and I am now more determined than ever to make sure that I am someone who you can be proud of and someone who you can look up to.

I would also like to dedicate this book to my father, Dexter G. Moore. Thank you for never giving up on me and always believing in me. Thank you for being a great father to me and a wonderful grandfather to Laya. Thank you for always being there for me, even when you didn't know how. Thank you for being my best friend. I love you, Old Man.

I would also like to dedicate this book to the man who will forever be considered the love of my life: DeAndre L. Cunningham. Not a day goes by that I don't appreciate you and everything you do for our little family. From your long days at work to your long nights as a father, I appreciate and love your nature of never giving up.

And to my big sister, La'Sheila Miller, aka Ducati, thank you for always being there when I need you. Thank you for always being my inspiration for a new book. Your crazy ass is the reason why my crazy ass is still writing. I love you always.

Last but not least, I would like to thank my family, too many to name. Thanks for always being there when needed. I know I have been a headache and sometimes a handful, but I appreciate y'all for loving me anyway.

And a Special Thanks to my Monet Presents Family. Y'all are fucking awesome. It feels good to finally be a part of a team with support, motivation, kindness, and wisdom. Thanks for accepting me.

Chapter One

Nitro

"What the fuck is going on?" I asked myself upon seeing my father's car parked in my driveway. Knowing that he would typically call before popping up only made me assume there was an emergency.

The door squeaked as I slowly opened it. I immediately saw the figure of a woman standing at the end of the hallway, looking around my shit as if it were a damn museum or something. With one hand gripped tightly on the gun at my waist, I slowly inched my way toward her. She never heard me approaching her as she stood silently in my living room. She was covered from head to toe in clothes that some would think were bedsheets. The only thing that I could see was a pair of piercing gray eyes when she turned around. Then I saw my father standing in a far corner of the room.

"Who the hell is this? And what the fuck is she wearing?" I asked my father as I glared at her.

My sudden outburst startled her as she jumped backward and looked in my father's direction with wide eyes. Before any more words were spoken, my father pulled me into the dining room.

"Pops, what the hell is going on?" I asked again.

"Maybe if you shut the fuck up for a second, I can tell your dumb ass," he spat.

I took a long look at him as I contemplated if I should remind him that he was standing in *my* house unannounced so I could ask whatever I wanted, but I decided against it. Even at 57 years old with a bad back, Willie "Moe" Johnson was a name that still put fear in the hearts of the toughest men on the streets.

"Don was killed the other night," he announced. It was then that I noticed the sadness in his eyes.

I instantly put my head down in condolence. I could now see that the death of his best friend was taking a toll on him mentally. Although they'd been friends since their sandbox days, I'd only met him in person a few times. While my father continued to build his empire in America, Don, on the other hand, went back to his country to build another. Like my father, I heard that Don was the type of man who only showed his face on special occasions. On those rare occasions that he did, it was either to give someone a promotion or a death sentence.

"I'm sorry, Pops, but that still don't explain the chick out there."

"He was murdered along with his wife and two other daughters. They don't know who did it, but from my angle, it looks like it was an inside job or at least someone who knew them personally. We made a vow when we were younger that if something were to happen to one of us, the other would look out for their family," he explained. "This is me fulfilling that promise."

"Why does she have to be here, though, Pops?" I asked. "LaToya is going to flip the fuck out if she finds another bitch up in here, a friend of the family or not."

"For one, don't use that word when referring to Myleena. She's family, and you will treat her that way. Two, whoever killed Don and his family might not be done, and they might want her dead as well. With everyone knowing how close Don and I were, my place would be the first place they come looking. I need her to be protected by any means necessary," he said sternly. "As for LaToya, that's a personal matter; this is family. You know that the family always comes first," he added.

"What about Ma?" I questioned. "If they're not done and try to take you out, don't you think they might try her too?"

"Believe me, son, yo' momma ain't always been the sweet little housewife she is today. Being with me as long as she has, she's learned just as much as I have on how to protect herself and knows what to do if worse comes to worst. Not to mention, she has bodyguards with her wherever she goes. As far as Myleena, who is here in your house, I'm still trying to piece that shit together before I make any moves."

"I'm sure you got plenty of places for this chick to crash at. Why here?"

"Are you questioning me?" he asked as he closed in the little bit of space that separated us.

The menacing glare he was giving me sent a chill to the very core of my soul, and I knew immediately to back down. Stepping back and putting my head down, I knew I had no choice but to obey my father's orders.

I closed my eyes and took a deep breath. Although I didn't know what I was walking into with having this girl at my place, I would stand ten toes down behind my father because, like he said, family always came first, no matter what. With that thought in my head, I followed my father back into the living room.

"Sorry about that"—he began as he placed his hands in his pockets—"Myleena, this is my son, Nitro," he said as he introduced us.

"Nice to meet you," I said, extending my hand to her.

She looked down at my hand for a few seconds before finally accepting it.

"Nice to meet you too," she replied.

I immediately noticed her strong, foreign accent and slightly broken English.

"You are safe here. Until I get everything situated, this will be home," Pops explained as he held her by the shoulders.

"Home?" she questioned with a puzzled look.

"Yes," he answered, "Nitro has spare bedrooms in the back. I'm sure he will have no problem helping you get settled," he answered as he looked back over at me, daring me to object.

"No," I interrupted, "if she has to be here, I already have a room prepared for her. It's toward the back of the house," I said as I picked up her bags. "Follow me."

It's true. I had plenty of rooms for her to stay in, but I figured the room in the back would suit her best. Not to mention, it would help me when I broke this shit down to LaToya.

She followed closely behind me as I led the way down the hallway. I stopped at the last room on the right. After opening the door, I stepped aside and allowed her to enter. Her face lit up as she scanned the huge bedroom, complete with a bathroom, sitting area, and a minibar. The silver glitter-style tiled flooring with black designs made the black stainless-steel bed frame stand out. It was definitely a room straight out of a magazine, and that was exactly what I wanted it to look like.

"This room is fit for a queen," she murmured as she ran her hand across the purple and black, fluffy and soft comforter set.

She continued to walk around and examine the room. As my eyes traveled down her slim frame, it was then that I noticed that this chick wasn't wearing any shoes.

"You don't have shoes?" I asked with raised eyebrows.

"Tradition is that we are not allowed to wear shoes inside the house," she answered over her shoulder. "We leave them at the door."

Although I couldn't stand bare feet, I couldn't help but notice her perfectly French-manicured toes. "Well, I guess we're gonna have to invest in some socks."

I shook my head as I took one last look at those beautiful gray eyes. *Well, it looks like I'm going to have to get li'l momma some house shoes,* I thought, because I wasn't too comfortable with people walking around my crib barefoot. Not even LaToya.

"Pops, what's the deal with her not wearing shoes? You know how I am about feet," I said to my father as we walked back toward the front of the house.

He said nothing, shook his head, and laughed as he strolled out the front door. Just as my father left, my phone began to ring. I immediately got a headache as LaToya's name and picture flashed across the screen.

"Yo," I answered.

"Where the fuck are you? I been waiting on yo' ass for a while."

I instantly regretted answering the phone. I was so distracted with the shit that had just fallen into my lap that I forgot that I had to pick her up from work. Not to mention that she knows nothing about the girl staying here. This ain't gonna sit too well with her.

"Fuck. I'm on my way," I said as I prepared to disconnect the call.

"Don't bother," she spat, smacking her lips together. "I already called an Uber. They picking me up from work and bringing me to your house," she replied with attitude before hanging up on me.

I needed a drink—better yet, I needed a quiet place to think. Knowing how erratic LaToya was when she was mad, I knew I didn't have time to sit and think of how to explain this situation to her. I had under thirty minutes before she would be at the door.

Chapter Two

Myleena

I looked around the place I would now be calling home, and I couldn't help the tears that came to my eyes.

"I'm sorry, Daddy. I promised you that I wouldn't cry."

I quickly swiped at the tear before it got the chance to fall. To take my mind off of the death of my family, I turned on the television and began to get settled in. When I finally finished, my stomach started to growl. Walking toward the kitchen, I heard the distinct sounds of people arguing.

"Who the fuck is that?" I heard a female ask.

Instead of a response, all I heard was the sound of a slammed door followed by more arguing. Although I wasn't born in America, and English wasn't my native language, my father was sure to teach it to me, at least what he thought was necessary for me to know. Not to mention, from all the music and movies I watched and liked to listen to, I picked up on their language and culture more quickly than most would have, but I knew I still had a lot to learn.

I opened the refrigerator and was disgusted by all the pork I saw. It only made me wonder what I would eat while I was here. Seeing that there was a bottle of cranberry juice and a bowl of fresh fruit, I shrugged as I grabbed it and walked over to the sink. Having a distinct feeling that someone was watching me, I turned around but was surprised when no one was there. Thinking it was just nerves from being in new surroundings, I quickly washed off the fruit and returned to the bedroom.

As I sat on the bed and nibbled on a grape, the only thing I could wonder about was what I would do in America. What was there to do? I was utterly alone and didn't know how to handle it. As much as I tried not to think about that night, it constantly replayed in my head.

It was a Saturday night, which meant that it was family night. Most of my dad's security was gone for the weekend. We sat in the living room watching television after an eventful but fun night of playing board games and laughing with one another.

"Myleena," my father called out as he sat beside my mother.

"Yes, Daddy?"

"I heard you got accepted into one of the best colleges in America. I'm so proud of you."

"Thanks, Daddy," I said nervously as I thought of the best possible way to ask my next question. I guess he could read my uneasiness as he cleared his throat before speaking again.

"And before you ask, no, you are not staying in the dormitories—too many bad influences. You will live in a private residence. Frank and Enrico will be with you at all times except during class, but just because they're not around doesn't mean they won't be close by."

My smile immediately disappeared as my father gave me the rundown on the rules and regulations of my soon-to-be new life in America.

"Why can't I live in the dorms like a normal student? You let Nabila," I pouted, but I instantly regretted men-

tioning my other sister. My younger sisters looked at each other with wide, fearful eyes, already knowing I had crossed a forbidden line.

"Yes, because I thought that I could trust her," he replied through gritted teeth.

I put my head down in shame and sadness as I thought about my other sister. She was the eldest of us all, but because of her choices in college, my father disowned her and washed his hands of her. Word around our small city was that not only did she give a man who wasn't of our religion her virginity, but she also became pregnant. Although she was in America when it happened, word spread quickly when it was about our people, especially with how high up in society my father was. Word quickly got back to my father about her actions, and he was just as fast when he rendered his verdict that she was no longer his daughter.

It was in our Pakistani custom that a woman is to be forever shamed and exiled for acts such as this and is disowned by the entire family as well as others in the same class ranking. It is said that the woman would forever be shunned by society, and her chances of marriage were doubtful. Any woman who would go against custom would spend the rest of their life as a whore. No matter how rich and powerful my father was or how much he loved my sister, he still honored our traditions. So, for the sake of our family's name and reputation, we were to act as if she never existed, and if anyone were to ask my father how many children he had, he would always say three instead of four.

"Myleena!" he shouted as I snapped from my thoughts. "Are you listening to me?" he asked when he saw me staring at the wall before me.

"Listen to your father," my mother chimed in as she took a sip of water.

"Yes, ma'am."

"Against my better judgment and at your mother's insistence, I'm not going to make you pay for the sins of your sister. I will allow you to live on campus, but you do understand my terms, correct?" he repeated.

"Yes, sir."

"And you do know what will happen if you disobey me, correct?"

"Yes, sir," I answered.

"Good. Frank and Enrico will still be around, but they won't be hovering over you," he said after a deep breath. "Don't make me regret this decision. I'm not sure if I'll be as lenient with you as I was with your sister."

"I won't," I replied with my head still down. "May I be excused, please?" I asked as I finally looked up at my parents.

I waited for my father to give me permission before I rose from my place on the floor. I hurriedly retreated to my wing of the house. As I walked down the halls of our mansion, I immediately hated the lifestyle my father provided us with. Although we were always given the best that money could buy, I longed to be normal. I envied the lifestyles that I saw others live on the television, being able to eat out whenever you wanted to, being able to shop wherever you wanted . . . just being able to be free. That was the lifestyle I wanted, but this was the life I was given.

With my father being the man he was, my life was sheltered and very well protected. I could barely go to the bathroom without a bodyguard knowing my every move or without them knowing just how many squares it took to wipe my ass correctly.

I stared at the wall for what seemed like hours as I thought of everything I would do with my new and less-sheltered life in America. But before long, the *sounds of bullets filled the air and scared me out of my thoughts as I was sitting on my bed. Knowing that my father didn't own any guns and knowing that our guards only used guns when necessary, I knew that danger had found its way into what was once called our safe haven.*

Instantly knowing the drill my father instilled in my head at an early age, I ran into the room next to mine. Putting in the new numbers that my father had me memorize, I entered the code, and the door opened. The code was changed often. I could feel the sweat forming on my forehead as I suddenly remembered to close the door tightly until I heard it click.

Until now, I had never had a reason to use this room, but I was now happy that my father thought of this as an escape plan. My father was a man who liked to be prepared for anything. "Prevent and prepare, not repent and repair." That statement alone was why he had rooms like these built on every wing of the house. A bulletproof room that had cameras that overlooked the entire house. It was a room that I had always been fascinated with since I was a child. In the words of my father, it was a room that couldn't be broken into. It was a safe haven within a safe haven.

Through the monitors, I saw my mother and both of my sisters gunned down and shot in their chests. I watched helplessly as I saw my father take two bullets to the chest as well. Even with blood streaming from the wounds, he was determined not to go down so easily as he yelled and looked around. I cried and screamed as he staggered his way over to where my mother and sisters were sprawled out on the floor before he finally fell to his knees.

The two intruders walked in behind a group of men toting guns. They walked through the hallways and shot the chefs and maids working over the weekend. Although

I wasn't sure if they were looking for me, I knew not to take any chances.

Tears continued to flood my vision as I replayed in my head the sight of my little sisters gasping for air. It was then that I glanced back over to the monitor and was able to see my father as he still clung to life. Even through the lens of the camera, I could still see the tears in his eyes as he held onto my mother's hand tightly while wiping the blood that still spilled from her mouth. My heart shattered as he kissed her one last time before her eyes finally closed. With his head merely inches above her chest, I knew that he was losing this battle as the killers just stared with their guns aimed at him. As if he knew that his time on earth was dwindling, he looked in the direction of the cameras. It was as if he knew I was where he told me to be if this ever happened.

"Don't cry," he mouthed. "Promise me that you won't cry. It's all a part of the game," he said before trying to hold his head up to defy the killers.

I nodded my head as if he could see me. His lips trembled as he grabbed the prayer beads that dangled from my mother's neck. Veins popped from his forehead as he mouthed a prayer. Tears poured as I closed my eyes and prayed with him. I prayed that God would have mercy on him. I knew the type of man that my father was, and I knew he wasn't perfect. Even though I knew what he did for a living, it didn't change the fact that he was my father and did what he had to do to provide for us and give us the best life he could.

Even though he told me not to cry, that didn't stop the tears already there. Then the figure of a woman in a masquerade mask walked over to him. She kicked him and forced him to turn over on his back. With her heeled boot in the center of my father's chest, she took a quick glance at my mother's corpse before returning her attention to my father.

With her back facing the camera, she took off her mask and placed the barrel of the gun on my father's head before she pulled the trigger.

I jumped from fear as his body convulsed from the pressure of the bullet as it penetrated his body. His eyes looked up to the ceiling as his fists clenched together for a few seconds before finally resting at his side. She then placed the mask back over her face before turning around. As she looked at the camera, her lips turned into a sinister yet beautiful smile before she waved at the cameras and walked away.

I wiped the tear that fell to my cheek as I pulled myself from that painful memory. Although I was hungry in the beginning, just thinking about the brutal death of my family ruined my appetite.

Music played softly in the background as I lay on the bed and stared out the bay-style window. I soon felt the presence of someone behind me. Turning around, I saw the shadow of what appeared to be a woman as she walked back down the hallway. My eyebrows shot up in confusion as I got up and walked toward the door. I was sure to keep quiet as I crept down the hall. I soon stopped at the bedroom entrance where the arguing had come from.

"So, not only is a bitch staying with you for an extended time, but she also went into the refrigerator and ate my damn fruit!" she yelled through the closed door.

Chapter Three

Nitro

"Seriously, Nitro, who the fuck is this bitch? And why the fuck does she think it's okay to walk freely into the kitchen and take food out of the refrigerator?"

"Watch your fucking mouth," I replied as I ran my hands down my face. "I told you the shit is complicated, but at the end of the day, she's family. So, don't fuck with her."

I paid no attention to her huffing and puffing and acting like the spoiled brat she was. Instead of feeding into her nonsense, I left her to her thoughts as I walked out of my bedroom and to my office. Frustrated wasn't even the word as I sat at my desk and pulled out my work phone. After reviewing future moves with a few of my top lieutenants, I clicked on my television and flipped the channel to the Sports Center.

My thoughts raced as the sportscaster went over the highlights of last night's game. Even with the day being almost over, that still didn't calm my headache.

"What are you doing in here?" LaToya asked as she walked in and closed the door behind her.

"Working," I replied with irritation. "What do you want?"

"I just wanted to apologize for how I was acting in the bedroom."

"Whatever, LaToya. Spit that shit to someone that don't know the real you."

"I'm sorry, baby. You know I just get crazy sometimes."

Looking in her direction, it was then that I saw that she was only wearing a pair of wine-red lace panties with a matching bra. That paired with a pair of black heeled boots. The lingerie complemented her mocha-colored skin perfectly as she stood next to the door. A part of me was pissed off at the fact that she was walking around like this, knowing that Myleena was here, but like I said, I knew LaToya, and I knew that she had an ulterior motive. Deep down, I knew she only did this to mark her territory. She wanted to show Myleena that I was hers, even though that was far from the truth.

"Like what you see?" she asked with a seductive smirk as she slowly walked over to me.

I didn't bother to respond as she pulled me away from my desk. A sexy smirk was plastered across her face as she slithered her body between my legs like a snake. In no time at all, her thick, plump lips were wrapped tightly around my dick. I grabbed a handful of her hair as she swallowed it. With grace, her head bobbed up and down on my nine inches.

"Hmm," she moaned in between her slurping and sucking.

One thing that I loved about LaToya was that although she ran her mouth, she also knew just how to use it. I allowed my mind to run freely as the sounds of her mouth blessing me filled my ears. Somewhere in between her sucking and slurping, her mouth was replaced with her already dripping-wet pussy. With her back facing me, I kept my eyes on her ass as it bounced against my legs. I grabbed a fistful of her hair as I yanked her head back. I wanted to see her face each time I rammed my dick into her.

"Oh, right there, baby. Yes," she moaned as she continued to bounce.

Within minutes she was creaming all over my dick. Moments later, I felt the throbbing in my dick, followed by a tingling sensation building. I pounded her walls until I felt myself nearing my peak. Just as I felt myself on the verge of exploding, she jumped off my inches and placed my dick back inside her warm, wet mouth.

"Yes, Zaddy," she moaned loudly just as I shot my load inside her mouth and down her throat.

I gathered myself as she pulled herself up from the floor. I looked up at her as she looked down at me with seduction etched on her face.

"Do you forgive me now?" she asked with her lips poked out.

"Yeah, I forgive you," I replied as I turned on my computer. "But I need you to do me a favor."

"And what's that?" she purred. "You ready for round two?"

"Nah," I answered. "I need you to take Myleena to the mall or something to get her some clothes and stuff," I said as I focused my attention on the television. "And be sure to get her some house shoes."

"You can't be serious," she replied with her hands folded across her chest. "You're *really* asking me to take the same bitch that's staying with you on a shopping spree?" she yelled.

"For one, I'm gonna need for you to lower your fucking voice in my house. Second, her name is Myleena. So, let that be the last time you refer to her as a bitch," I threatened. "Understand?"

With my eyes glued to my computer screen, I could still see her as she pouted like a kid, but honestly, I didn't care about her attitude.

"Fine. I'll do it, but she better not expect me to hold her hand. I'm not a fucking babysitter," she said as she smacked her lips together and walked to the door.

"Call Ace and tell him to pull the car around. There are a few stacks under the bed in the other spare bedroom. Grab how much you'll need and have fun," I instructed as she slammed the door behind her.

I let out a long, exhausted breath. LaToya could definitely be a handful, and sometimes, I wondered if she was truly worth the headache she was becoming. Throughout our years together, my mother constantly asked if I was in love with her or even loved her. Each time she asked, all I could say was that I had love for LaToya. She was definitely a dime and would be the picture of any nigga's fantasy. I just wasn't sure if she was the kind of woman who would hold a nigga down and make wifey. Again, I had love for her. I just didn't know if it was true love or if the so-called love would even last.

"I guess only time will tell," I said as I leaned back in my chair and thought of where my life was taking me.

Chapter Four

LaToya

I rolled my eyes as I walked beside the same bitch who would be sharing the same space with my man. With Ace trailing behind us, I looked over at the bitch and couldn't help the chuckle that escaped my glossy lips. I was dressed in nothing but the best . . . a black Gucci dress that hugged my thick hips and showcased my thick and toned thighs and legs. It was perfectly paired with my favorite pair of silver, diamond-encrusted Steve Madden stilettos.

As I thought of myself, I looked at her and saw absolutely no reason to feel threatened by her stealing my man. Dressed looking like a black ninja, she was covered from head to toe. I strutted my stuff like the bad bitch that I was as I led the way into the Gucci store.

"Here, try this on," I instructed as I threw a dress in her direction.

She looked at the dress as if it were covered in shit before shifting her gaze back over to me.

"Oh no," she said while shaking her head. "I can't wear this," she replied while handing the dress back to me.

"And why not?" I asked, slightly offended only because I was wearing the exact same dress.

"It's not my style. Besides, it's against my religion to show off skin in public."

"Well, you may find it hard to believe, but it's going to be a hell of a lot harder to find anything fashionable if that's the style you're aiming for."

"Believe it or not, what I have on is Gucci," she informed me. "Custom made . . . just for me."

"Well, I don't see how you're gonna catch a man when you're dressing like that."

"Not really looking for one."

"I know you miss dick."

"No."

"You can't be serious," I answered, sipping my water.

"Can't miss something you've never had," she replied as she walked away from me.

I damn near spit out the water in Ace's face at the mention of her still being a virgin. I've never met anyone over the age of 16 who was still a virgin. That fact alone only made me wonder how old she actually was.

I followed her as she shifted through the different racks. Although I wasn't entirely sure what she was looking for, I could only assume she was looking for more of the bedsheets she called clothes. She continued to browse through the racks until she came upon the last one. As she reached the last article of clothing, she looked over at me before leaving it on the rack.

As we headed to the front of the store, I couldn't help but notice that she hadn't found anything. Where she had nothing in her hands, I had plenty in mine. Although I did not need any new clothes, I would have been a damn fool to pass up a shopping spree on Nitro's dime. After paying for the items I wanted, I handed my bags to Ace. We walked into store after store, and still, she saw nothing to wear. After the seventh store, I had completely given up. I'd be lying if I said that I wasn't fed up with her shallow and modest ass.

"Ace, I'm ready to go," I said as I handed him the last of my bags. "Go pull the car around to the entrance. We'll meet you around there in about five minutes."

"But she hasn't found anything to wear," he mentioned. "This shopping spree was for her, not you."

"And she's not going to find anything but them damn house slippers that I had to pick out for her. Have you or have you *not* noticed that we've been in damn near ten stores, and she hasn't found even a pair of fucking socks. I got better shit to do than just to walk around looking for clothes that look like sheets," I yelled.

"It's okay," she replied in her thick accent. "I'm ready to go anyway. I've never been a fan of shopping."

"Are you sure?" Ace asked, completely ignoring me.

"Yes," she replied with a smile.

With her say-so, Ace smiled before walking toward the exit. I rolled my eyes at her as I swished my hips and walked over to the mall exit. Looking behind me, I made sure that she was following, but upon looking back, I saw that she had stopped walking and was now looking in the far corner of the wall.

"What are you looking at?" I asked with attitude as I looked in the same direction as she was.

"Nothing," she answered, snapping her head back in my direction.

I couldn't hide my disdain for her presence, and I wasn't happy until we were finally back inside Ace's car and headed back to Nitro's place. I finally found solace as I turned on my Pandora and leaned my head back. Monica sang her heart out about not giving it up on the first night. Even though I liked the song, I just couldn't jig with it. Unlike Monica, I'd fuck a nigga on the first night and not have a second thought about it. That's how I got Nitro. In fact, my pussy grip and head skills are what has been keeping him around for all these years. And I planned on keeping him for many years to come.

Chapter Five

Myleena

Two Months Later . . .

"Thanks for taking me to the store," I said to Ace as he stood posted by the door.

"No problem at all. Just let me know what you need, and I'll get it done," he replied with a wink.

I stood by the stove as I toasted up some flat bread. It was starting to smell like home as I whipped up some chicken karahi. I was craving something spicy, and as appetizing as American foods looked, they didn't compare to what I could whip up.

"Whatever you're over there cooking, it sure as hell smells good as hell," Ace said from across the room.

"Excuse me?" I said in confusion.

"Your cooking smells good as hell," he repeated.

"Umm, I'm sorry. It's almost finished," I replied as I tried to fan away the smoke.

"No need to be sorry."

"You said my food smells like hell . . . That doesn't sound like a compliment."

If I were confused initially, I was more than confused now as he began to laugh at me.

"What's funny?" I asked.

"When someone says that your food smells good as hell, that *is* a compliment, believe me. It's been a while since someone has been in that kitchen. So, I know when something smells good," he said as he continued to laugh.

"LaToya doesn't cook?"

"Hell naw," he replied before laughing. "All she know how to do is pick up a phone and order takeout."

I was no longer in a state of confusion. I was now in a state of embarrassment. I still hadn't managed to learn the American slang. It was as if everything they said or did was the exact opposite of what it really was, completely confusing. None of the American shows that I was watching helped me much, but like I said, I was still learning.

"Umm, thank you," I replied, turning back toward the stove.

Ten minutes later, I finished cooking. With Ace chowing down on his food, I sat across from him and began eating. To say that I enjoyed one of my country's signature dishes would have been putting it lightly. I was in complete heaven as the crispy but spicy chicken made love to my taste buds. It instantly made me think of my mother and how, every Saturday, she'd be whipping up a buffet fit for an army.

"Damn, you can throw down in the kitchen," Ace commented.

"What does that mean?" I asked before stuffing another piece of chicken into my mouth.

"It's a compliment," he replied, laughing and shaking his head at me.

Even with him laughing, he never stopped stuffing his face. Minutes later, the front door burst open. Ace and I immediately locked eyes as we heard Nitro and LaToya arguing, something that I'd noticed they did on a regular. For the life of me, I just couldn't figure out why he chose to be with her. In my opinion, she was rude, self-centered, and completely selfish. Although from what I could see,

Nitro was no saint either, but he still didn't deserve to be with someone so mean and self-entitled.

Even though I had these thoughts in my head, I was sure never to speak them aloud, at least not to anyone other than Ace, who has given me the history of LaToya and Nitro's past together. Much to my surprise, Ace disliked her almost as much as I did. During the months of my stay here, there had been plenty of times when I would hear her talking about me, whether it was to Nitro or to someone she was speaking with on the phone. It didn't matter what I did. She always had something negative to say about me.

"What the fuck is that smell?" she complained as she walked into the kitchen.

"Myleena cooked," Ace answered as he licked his fingers before winking at me again.

"Well, it looks like shit," she commented while peeking under the lids of the pots.

"LaToya, shut yo' ass up and go to the room," Nitro commanded as he entered the kitchen, causing Ace to laugh. "Always talking shit about something that don't involve you." He continued to fuss with his phone pressed against his ear.

"Shut yo' ass up, Ace," she screamed as she did what she was told.

But Ace continued to laugh as he stared at me before smirking. I smiled back at him before turning my attention to my plate.

"What is this shit?" Nitro asked as he looked through the pots. "It smells good."

"It's chicken karahi," I replied.

Without another word, he placed his phone in his pocket, walked over to the cabinet, and pulled out a plate. I was amazed as well as shocked as he piled a plate of what looked like it was meant for two. Thinking that he had grabbed a serving for him and LaToya, I was even more surprised when he sat right next to me.

For the next few minutes, all that could be heard were the sounds of chewing and Nitro and Ace's forks scraping their plates. I felt a sense of happiness wash over me as they enjoyed the same dishes that my mother and father used to cook for me, but as I looked at them munch, I couldn't help but laugh at them.

"What's so funny?" they asked together while staring at each other.

"The two of you," I answered.

"What about us?" Ace asked.

"Y'all are eating with forks," I replied while still laughing.

It was then that they looked over at my plate and saw that instead of eating with utensils, I was scooping up my food with pieces of flat bread.

"In my country, it's rare that you use forks and spoons. We use bread."

"Well, you're in America now, baby," Nitro said. "And in America, we eat with silverware. Speaking of America, my father told me you will start school next week."

"Yes," I answered.

"Do you need anything?"

"I already handled that," Ace spoke.

"Good looking out, Ace," Nitro replied. "What are you thinking of taking up?" he asked as he looked back at me.

"I always wanted to be a doctor, but I've also been looking into law."

"I think you should get into culinary," Ace said as he took another spoonful of food.

"It tastes better with bread," I retorted.

"We'll see about that," they both said as they snatched up pieces of bread and scooped their food up with it.

"Damn, Nitro, I think she's on to something," Ace replied as he grabbed another piece of bread off of the plate in the middle of the table.

They continued to munch on the food, and we finished the rest of our meal in peace and silence . . . that was, until a still-upset LaToya stomped her way into the kitchen just as we finished.

"That was a damn good meal," Nitro said as he took his plate to the sink. "It was definitely different than what I would normally eat. I might have to get you to teach me that recipe."

"I'd be happy to," I replied, smiling as I grabbed Ace's and my plates and walked them over to the sink.

"I couldn't tell," LaToya said smartly as she stood at the kitchen entrance with her hands on her hips. "If it look like dog shit and smell like dog shit . . . I don't see the need for a recipe. Just take yo' ass to the source."

"LaToya, there yo' ass go again . . . talking when ain't nobody said shit to yo' ass," Nitro spat. "At least she cooks and cleans up after herself. More than what I can say about *yo'* ass. Got the nerve to talk shit about someone cooking, but yo' ass ain't never even touched a damn pot and don't know how to make shit else but noodles and canned ravioli and pizza rolls that still be cold in the middle."

Now completely embarrassed, I smiled on the inside as her face turned a bright shade of red, but instead of replying or walking back to the room, she walked straight to the front door and slammed it shut behind her.

"I guess you really pissed her off now," Ace commented.

"Man, I'm getting tired of her nagging ass," he replied as he looked at me.

For some reason, I always felt smaller than I really was whenever he looked at me, but at the same time, whenever our eyes locked, it would cause my heart to beat ten times faster than usual.

"So, what are your plans for the rest of the day?" Nitro asked me.

"No plans," I replied nervously.

"Well, I noticed you didn't get anything the last time I told LaToya to take you shopping. So, how about we head out and see if we can find you something to wear to the party."

"Party?"

"Yeah. My dad is throwing a party for my mother's fiftieth birthday in a few weeks. You're invited," he announced.

"I don't think that'll be a good idea."

"It will be. You can be my date."

"I *really* don't think that'll be a good idea," I said, now more resistant than before. "LaToya already doesn't like me . . . That will only make her more furious."

"She won't be there. She's not invited. Now, go get dressed. I'll be outside waiting in the car. No excuses, no exceptions."

Chapter Six

Willie Moe Johnson

I racked my brain continuously as I replayed the security tapes from Don's place. Men with masks stormed through every room in the house, firing at anything that moved, but there was something about one of them that stood out from the rest. Unlike the others, this figure was a woman. She slowly stalked the halls until she came to the family room.

I was in shock as she single-handedly annihilated the man I had the pleasure of calling my best friend, my brother. My tears threatened to fall as the tape continued to play, showing the army of killers shooting Don's wife and his youngest daughters before turning the gun on him.

But each time that I replayed the video, something stuck out. The masked woman was familiar with the house. She knew exactly where to go. I observed how she moved and walked through the halls that led directly to Myleena's room. I noticed how she walked to the door and tried to push in the code to open it. I saw her retry it a few times before finally becoming frustrated. But before she left, she was sure to look into the cameras before waving and walking away.

"Who are you?" I asked myself as the mysterious woman stared up at the camera. That one question plagued my mind as she turned around and walked down the halls and out of the house, but just as the woman disappeared, other doubts and questions plagued my mind. Was Myleena a part of the destruction of her family? Did she have something to do with the murder of my best friend and the rest of his family?

"Hey, baby. What are you doing here?" Valentina asked as she appeared behind me.

"Nothing."

"Still looking over those tapes?" she asked, massaging my shoulders.

"Yeah. I still can't believe he's gone."

"We all know the consequences that we face in this game. Do you think I haven't spent my fair share of nights worrying about you? I knew the man I fell in love with, and I knew what we were risking," she whispered. "I knew there might be a cost when I decided to be with you."

"Yeah. We all know the chances of this shit, but you never plan for it to happen."

"And I never want it to happen to you or our son, but I can't stop him from doing what's in his blood to do. His momma was a hustler, and his daddy was a hustler; it's inevitable. All I can do is thank the Lord that you're finally hanging up this life," she said as she kissed my freshly shaved head.

I looked up into her shimmering hazel eyes, and it was at this time that I remembered why I fell in love with her all those years ago. She was just like me. Most women in our day just wanted to snag the nigga making the most money, but from the first time that I met Valentina, I knew that she was different. She didn't just want to spend the money; she was in the trenches with me, helping me make the money. When we got the money, she didn't just spend it on bullshit that didn't mean shit once it was bought. She went to school and invested our money.

She turned a thousand-dollar-a-week hustle into a multibillion-dollar-a-week business. A business that only dealt with the most elite distributors in the country. Not only was I a part of the biggest and most elite drug empire in the Northern Hemisphere, but we also had nightclubs as well as a few barbershops and laundromats. I wasn't lying when I said my wife was more than just a cute face. My baby had brains to go with it. "Behind every strong man is an even stronger woman" was a phrase she often spoke to me.

"Yeah, me too. I can only hope that I've taught our son enough for him to continue to build on what I've already started."

"I'm sure you have. Look at that boy," she said with a smile. "What man do you know who can make his first million dollars by flipping just one kilogram of cocaine?" she asked with a laugh.

Knowing that my son was a true hustler, I couldn't help but feel a sense of pride. A lot of niggas in the game thought they could be hustlers just by watching a few movies like *New Jack City* or *Belly*. This hustling shit only came easily and naturally to a few, and I was proud to say that my son was one of them.

"Yeah," I said with a smile. "I think you're right."

Chapter Seven

Myleena

My heart raced as I sat in the passenger seat of Nitro's car, but thankfully, my hijab covered most of my face. Although I've been living with him for a little over two months, for some reason, I still became nervous whenever he was around me. It didn't matter how often we had conversations or how much we were beginning to have in common, I just couldn't control my racing heartbeat when he was near.

"So, what type of music are you into?" he asked as he glanced at me as we approached a red light.

"A little bit of everything," I answered nervously. "I generally like music by Trey Songz and Beyoncé, but everything of American culture was pretty much forbidden in Pakistan."

"So, you've never really done anything?"

"Not really. My father always kept his eyes on me."

"I guess living here really is different from what you're used to then."

"It is. When he was on trips, sometimes I could sneak and watch a few American shows," I replied with a hidden smile.

"Oh yeah?" he asked. "Shows like what?"

"*Love* and *Hip-Hop*, but over the past few weeks, you've shown me a few things," I said with a smile.

"Well, that's good. Them reality shows seem so typical," he laughed. "I have yet to meet a female who wasn't into *Love* and *Hip-Hop*. Me, personally, I don't see the point in it. It's all just surrounded by petty drama and fake love."

"I guess for me, it was just seeing how free and happy other people's lives were. I envied their lives," I replied with a shrug of my shoulders.

"I don't see what's so glamorous about it."

I was grateful when we finally pulled up to the same mall that LaToya and I were at previously. I felt so out of place as I walked behind Nitro. Covered from head to toe in my all-gray ensemble, I definitely stood out from the other women who were wearing little to nothing as they carried multiple bags in their hands. Even with my hijab almost covering my eyes, I could still see the girls as they practically drooled at the sight of Nitro.

I blushed as he waved at some and winked at others. At that moment, I wondered how he met LaToya. Although I didn't know much about either, they just didn't seem to match. Where he was silent, she was what his mother often referred to as a loudmouthed wench. Although I had only met his mother a few times, from what I could see, she was a very nice and soft-spoken woman, but just as she was soft-spoken, she was also stern with her words. I could see that she truly loved Nitro and wanted the best for him. She looked at him the same way that my mother used to look at my sisters and me.

"So, what name brands are you interested in?" Nitro asked as he turned to face me.

"You sound like LaToya," I replied with a sarcastic smile. "She asked me that same question the last time we were here."

"My bad. It's just hard to help someone if you don't know what they like."

"What exactly do I need to get all dressed up for?"

"I've told you. My mother is turning 50, and my father has planned a party for her. You're going to be my plus-one," he replied with a smile.

"Why isn't LaToya going with you?" I couldn't help but ask. "She's your girlfriend . . . right?"

"Yeah, but I've already told you she wasn't invited," he laughed. "Her and my mother don't quite get along."

"Really?" I asked with surprise. "And you're still with her?"

"Yeah. As you can see, I don't really go by no one else's rules but my own."

"But with them both being major parts of your life, how do you juggle them?"

"They tolerate each other for me, but with this being a major night for my mom, it was decided that it would be best for this to be an event she missed. Now, back to you and your wardrobe, what do you like? Because, like I've said before, it's kind of hard to shop for someone if you don't know what they like."

"Understandable, but this is pretty much all that I'm used to," I said as I made a gesture toward my current attire. "It's all I know, and it's a sin to show more skin."

"Really?" he asked with big eyes.

"Yes. My husband is The only person who should see my skin, body, or hair."

"You're married?"

"No. It's just tradition that I remain pure and untouched until marriage. I don't see that happening anymore."

It was then that I felt myself becoming more emotional the more I spoke. It was my parents' responsibility to decide the man that I was to marry, but with both of my parents gone and no known relatives, I was basically on my own. I didn't even know that a tear had fallen until Nitro was wiping away the tear that was now on at the tip of my nose.

"I'm okay," I replied as I backed away from him and sat on a nearby bench.

I closed my eyes as I tried to control my breathing. On some days, I felt like I was getting better knowing that my family was gone. At other times, I felt like I would never get over it.

"I know that I don't know you," he began, "and I won't pretend to. I don't know the pain of losing parents, but this is your chance to live your life . . . your way."

More tears streamed down my face the more that he spoke to me. Deep down, I knew that he was right. No matter how hard I tried to deny it, I knew that there were things that my parents believed in that I didn't. Most of all, I knew that there were things that I wanted to do in life that they would never have let me do.

"I can't just dishonor them and leave all of their beliefs behind."

"I'm not saying that you have to. All I'm saying is use this as a chance to do right by yourself."

A few minutes passed of just us staring at each other before a smile finally graced his face, forcing a smile to spread across mine as well. It was at this time that I saw how attractive he was. Maybe it was more than just his looks that made LaToya crazy about him. Perhaps it was his heart of gold.

"How about this? How about we change up your wardrobe just a little bit? I want you to be comfortable at home. So, we gonna go into a few stores and pick you out a few things. If we see anything you can wear for the party, we'll get that too."

"That sounds like a lot of money. I'm not sure how I'll ever be able to pay you back. My father didn't leave anything behind."

"Don't worry about it. I'll cover the tab," he joked as he took me by the hand.

I followed behind him as he led the way through the shopping mall. A look of confusion covered my hidden face as we walked into an unfamiliar store. I couldn't describe the weird sensation that took over me as a woman walked over to where we were. I stood helplessly as Nitro looked over my body before turning back to the saleswoman and rattling off some numbers.

"What were those numbers?" I asked once the lady was out of earshot.

"Your measurements."

"Measurements?" I questioned.

"At least estimates," he said with a smile.

"How are you able to guess my size just by looking?"

"Let's just say that I've had my fair share of seeing women."

I couldn't help but blush again under my hijab from his comment. As I stared at him from under my hood, I couldn't help but wonder just how many women he's "seen." About three hours later, we finally walked out of the mall and to the car.

I giggled as Nitro fumbled with the multiple bags in his hands as well as his keys. The women who walked by us gawked at him, trying desperately to get his attention, but he remained unfazed and unbothered. After placing most of the bags in the backseat and the rest in the trunk, we got into his car and pulled out of the parking lot.

I leaned my head back and relaxed as my body melted into the heated leather. Somewhere during the smooth ride, I closed my eyes and dozed off.

"Hey, wake up," I heard Nitro call out as I felt a hand brush against my leg.

The sudden feeling of someone touching me caused my eyes to pop open as I quickly sat up in my seat and looked out the window.

"What?" I asked in a panicked tone. "What's going on? Where are we?"

"Come on," he answered shortly before getting out of the car and walking over to my side.

The sun was beaming down on his light caramel complexion as he looked down at me with a smile. Taking me by the hand, he again led the way into a building.

"What are we doing here?" I asked again just as a woman approached us.

"We're here to get you a phone," he answered.

"Is there anything that I can help you with today?" the lady asked as she looked from me to him.

"We're looking to get her a phone," Nitro replied as he gestured to me. "What do you recommend?"

"The LG Stylo 5 is the most sophisticated phone we have on the floor right now," she began with a smile. "It has a great memory and excellent picture quality . . . not to mention internet speed."

"We'll take it," he said while not once taking his eyes away from his phone.

The lady winked at him and smiled over at me before walking away.

"What do I need a phone for?" I asked as I followed him to the cash register, where the lady stood and retrieved a phone from one of the display cases. "I rarely go anywhere, and when I do, I'm always with someone with a phone."

"It's for 'just in case' purposes. So, please, don't argue. Besides, it's unusual for Americans not to own a cell phone."

"But I'm not an American," I argued.

"You are now," he announced as he reached into his back pocket and pulled out a tiny booklet with my name and picture inside.

Tears immediately appeared as my hands brushed across the leatherlike material.

"I didn't take the naturalization test," I said, still in shock. "I thought that was mandatory before citizenship."

"It is," he replied. "But my father and I were able to pull a few strings with a few people. So, congratulations. You are now a citizen of the United States, but with Trump being in office, I don't see how good of a decision this was."

"He won't be for long," I joked back.

To say that I was still in shock by the news of my new-found citizenship would have been an understatement. I continued to run my fingers over my name and picture as I tried to gather my thoughts. Although it was always in my father's plan to get citizenship, it was only going to be temporary. This, however, was permanent. Without me knowing it, I soon found myself speaking.

"I know that a thank-you doesn't mean much, nor does it compare to all that you and your father have done for me, but I still want you to know that I greatly appreciate it," I said as I swiped away at a tear as it fell from my eye.

"Don't worry about it," he replied. "Like I said, it's a new beginning for you. Here's a phone for your new beginning," he said as he handed it to me a few minutes after the lady slid it over the table.

I smiled as I took the phone that was twice as big as my hand.

"I've already programmed my number in there. So, if you ever need me when I'm not around, just call me."

"Thank you," I replied.

After passing me the bag that held some phone accessories, we walked out of the phone store and back to his car. I placed the phone into my bag and put it on the floor as Nitro pulled away from the curb and down the street. About twenty minutes later, we were pulling back into the drive-in garage of his house.

"We didn't find the dress for your mother's party," I mentioned as I looked at him.

"I'm taking care of that right now," he replied before taking his phone from his pocket and placing it to his ear.

I peered out the window and tried not to listen to him as he spoke on the phone. Luckily, he only said a few words before hanging up and placing the phone back into his pocket.

"I have someone coming to make your dress. They'll be here within the hour."

We entered his house, and he helped me carry the bags to my room. The television played in the background as I unpacked the newly bought items Nitro had purchased for me. Occasionally, a look of confusion would wash over my face as I came across multiple items. In my country, women were always to wear dresses and never pants, but I soon learned that women wearing pants was a normal thing here.

Although this would take some time to get used to, I was ready to do what Nitro had suggested. I was ready to start living my life for me, the way that I wanted to. And I was about to start living my life the American way.

About thirty minutes later, someone knocked at the door, followed by a squeaking sound of it being opened. I was relieved to see that it was none other than Nitro, followed by another man. I stood back as they entered the room.

"Myleena, this is my boy, Donny," he said as he introduced us. "He's one of the best designers in New York."

"*One of the best?*" he asked, shocked, with a medium-sized suitcase rolling behind him. "I am *the best,* hun-ty," he replied with a snap of his fingers.

I couldn't stop the laugh that escaped my lips as I looked at Donny. He put me in the mind of Mister Rayy from *Love* and *Hip-Hop.*

"So, I was informed that you were invited to the famous Valentina Johnson's fiftieth birthday bash."

"Yes," I replied in a low voice as I kept my eyes on Nitro.

"Well, have no fear. Donny is here, and he will make you look *fierce*," he replied as he snapped his fingers again.

"I'll be downstairs if you need me," Nitro said as he walked toward the door.

"Only thing I'll need from you is my check and an apple martini, shaken, not stirred," he giggled. "What about you, chile?" he asked, returning his attention to me.

"I don't drink."

"Don't drink?" he asked appalled with a snap of his neck. "Hang with me a li'l more, and that'll change. You can close the door now. It's time for some girl time."

Nitro's phone rang as he closed the door. My nerves were getting the best of me as Donny walked around me. He eyed me the same way that Nitro did earlier while we were at the mall. But before long, a smile appeared.

"Girl, I'm gonna make you the baddest bitch at the party, even badder than Mrs. Johnson."

I remained quiet as he pranced over to his suitcase and unzipped it. He looked like a kid on Christmas Day as he rushed over to me with a tape measure in one hand and different shades of fabric in the other.

"You have a flawless figure, gorgeous hair, and beautiful eyes. Are those contacts?" he asked with squinted eyes.

"No. These are my real eyes."

"Well, *excuse* me. So, this is what I'm thinking . . ." he said as he took out a dark shade of fabric and held it against my skin. "Nitro has told me what your preferences are . . . but I'm going to need for you to trust me."

"Okay," I replied as I closed my eyes.

I took slow, deep breaths as he measured my arms and legs, followed by my waist. The more he measured me, the more scared I became. Finally, I sat on my bed, and he sat at my desk and sketched my dress. When he was finished and showed me the drawing, my mouth dropped to the floor. My dad would be rolling over in his grave if he were to see the dress that I would be wearing at this party.

"Here's to a new beginning," I said as I gave Donny my nod of approval.

Chapter Eight

LaToya

I was fuming as I sat on the stool and stared at Nitro. I glared in his direction with rage and envy as he got measured for a suit for his mother's fiftieth birthday party. The more I looked at him, the angrier I became at the fact that I wasn't invited.

"What is it, LaToya?" Nitro asked as he stood in front of the mirror while the tailor's assistant measured the length of his arms. "Yo' ass been pouting the entire time we've been here. What the fuck is your problem?"

"This," I yelled, standing up. "You're going to a party that *I'm* not invited to. That's fucked up."

"How is it fucked up? You know that you and my mom don't get along. So, don't act like you're surprised."

"We might not get along, but *I'm* your woman. You're supposed to defend me. *I'm* supposed to be the one on your arm."

I continued to glare at him as he pinched the bridge of his nose, which he often did when he was upset. I knew he was having difficulty keeping his composure, but I couldn't have cared less at this time. He was so busy caring about his mother—but what about me?

"LaToya, this night is about my mother. Not me and not you. You weren't invited. Get over it."

"Whatever," I spat as I sat back down.

My blood was slowly simmering as he constantly looked down at his phone. Usually, he was never on his phone unless it concerned business, and even that was only for a few minutes since he never liked to discuss business over the phone. But lately, I'd noticed that he was on it much more, and most of the time, he would laugh.

"What's so funny?" I asked through narrowed eyes.

"What?" he asked as he stared at me through the mirror.

"You heard me," I replied with my hands folded over my chest. "You never have your phone in your hand this much, but now, suddenly, you can't keep it in your pocket. Not only that, but you also keep laughing. So, what is it?" I asked as I jumped up again and walked toward him.

"LaToya, back up."

"No. I want to know what's so funny. I like to laugh just as much as the next person. So, let me see," I yelled as I tried to grab his phone.

"If you don't sit yo' ass down, I'ma knock yo' ass through that wall," he threatened through clenched teeth.

His sudden change in demeanor scared the lady measuring the length of his arms. I got a sick pleasure from seeing her sprinting toward the door leading to the store's back room.

I then rolled my eyes as I turned away from him and walked back over to the chair. I folded my arms back across my chest just as Donny walked out.

"Found it!" he announced gayly as he revealed a deep shade of red-colored fabric. "This would be perfect, especially for the occasion. So festive," he said with a snap of his fingers.

"Donny, you know that I only wear black. What's up with this red?" Nitro asked as he looked at the red with disgust.

"Trust me," he winked. "Besides, if you always only wear black, what's the point of buying a new suit for every function?" he asked sarcastically.

"I never wear the same suit twice," Nitro answered smartly. "Besides, if I didn't buy a suit for every party, I doubt you would have the funds to live as nice as you do or had the funds to start this boutique. So, you think I should stop?"

"Of course not. Didn't you know that no shade of black is the same? There's always one lighter or darker than the rest, kinda like men. No two are the same," he squealed. "Besides, I just put a new Rolls-Royce on layaway."

"Gay ass," I spat under my breath.

I couldn't help but shake my head. I couldn't stand Donny's gay ass. Other than his mother and father, Donny was the only person who didn't have to watch how he spoke to Nitro. Even with me being his girlfriend for the past seven years, I still had to tiptoe around specific topics and could only use certain words when speaking to him.

"Are we almost done?" I asked, growing impatient as I walked to the mirror and admired my coke-bottle figure. "Unlike you, we have other things to do. You just measured his arms last month. I doubt that they grew much since then."

"And unlike you, I'm a perfectionist," Donny spat with a roll of his eyes. "Everything must be perfect for this night. I'll be damned if I see any of my clients looking out of place—not if I have to witness it."

My neck snapped in his direction as I looked from him and back to Nitro.

"Witness?" I asked through narrowed eyes. "You were invited?"

"Of course I was," he bragged with a smile. "Who do you think helped Mr. Johnson coordinate the colors, pick the cake . . . You know, *gay* shit like that," he spat back to me before turning his attention back to Nitro.

"I can't believe this shit," I screamed as I rushed over to Nitro. "*He's* been invited to the party, and *I'm* not? Nitro, *do* something about this."

"Oh, you weren't invited?" Donny asked sarcastically. "Such a shame. I would have loved to see you there."

"Whatever. I'm ready to leave. So, can we speed this bullshit up?"

"I'm not gonna rush a damn thing," Donny yelled back as he threw his material to the floor. "If you got someplace to be, use both of them twigs that you call legs and walk."

"Nitro!"

"LaToya, either you can sit yo' ass down, or you can call a cab or Uber, but I'm getting tired of yo' shit."

I rolled my eyes once more as I stomped back to the chair. I don't know what was up with Nitro, but this bullshit that he was putting me through was getting out of control. As I sat there and scrolled through my phone, I often looked over to Donny and found him looking at me before smiling. It was as if he were taking his time with this damn measuring shit on purpose. Fuck him wanting it to be perfect. The way I saw it, he lived to torment me.

"Done," Donny finally announced after what felt like an eternity. "I'm going to start on this right now. It will be finished by the weekend."

"You sure you can get it done that soon?" Nitro asked. "It normally takes you a few weeks."

"Well, with the money you've been spending, I was able to hire a few extra hands to help. So, like I said, give me a few days, and I'll deliver yours when I deliver Myleena's."

"Sounds good," Nitro replied as he stepped down from the platform.

"*Myleena?* Myleena is going?"

"She was invited," Nitro replied without a care.

I couldn't describe the feeling that was building up in my chest. If there was a word that could describe every hateful feeling in the world, that was the way I was feeling. In the beginning, I was angry because I wasn't invited. But now, I was pissed more at the fact that this new bitch was invited, and I wasn't. I took a few deep breaths before I followed Nitro out the shop door and to his car.

My evil glare only intensified as Nitro put his key in the ignition and pulled away from the curb. I was spewing hate as I listened to him as he rapped to the lyrics of Kevin Gates as if he didn't have a care in the world. With his phone perched on the dashboard, I saw him as he scrolled through his text messages.

What was once a tiny rage was now a full-blown fire as I saw him scroll to his last received message. Like my momma once said, it doesn't matter if a bitch needed glasses on a regular basis. When it comes to her man's phone, a blind bitch will have 20/20 vision when it comes to a bitch texting her man. Even from a few feet away, I could read Myleena's name and number as clear as day.

"Bitch," I said to myself. "That conniving, little terrorist-bombing bitch."

Chapter Nine

Unknown

My heels clicked across the marble floor as I paced my conference room. I was getting so tired of these incompetent niggas. It didn't matter how specific or descriptive I was at the tasks that I assigned them. These niggas would always find a way to come up short or empty-handed.

"How do you know that bitch was even in there when we shot up the shit?" Duke asked.

"Watch your fucking mouth," I spat. "And what the fuck did I tell you about questioning me?" I asked as I whipped out my .22 and aimed it at his head.

Beads of sweat immediately formed on his forehead and dripped from his eyebrow to his bottom lip. I laughed at how his eyes grew as big as saucers and his lips trembled from fear. An evil smile came to my face, and I enjoyed the sight of his hands shaking as they rested at his side.

"Boss," he said with a quivering and shaky voice.

My smile stayed plastered on my face as I slowly turned my head around and looked at the big, burly figure sitting in a chair at the head of the table.

"Boss," I mocked.

I gazed at my man as he looked at me with lustful eyes. The same qualities that most men found scary about me, he found sexy. The same techniques that I used to kill niggas in the streets, he used to pleasure me in the bedroom. Fuck that BDSM and *Fifty Shades of Grey* kind of shit. We were into the shit that caused that real pain. That kind of shit that leaves bruises and to see who drew the first-blood type of pain.

"I ain't got shit to do with that," he said with a shrug of his shoulders as he looked on. "A real man knows not to ever go against the words of his queen."

"You hear that, motherfucker?" I yelled through clenched teeth as my grip around the handle of my gun got tighter. "Don't *ever* question my word, and don't *ever* try to get him to go against me because you'll fail every time," I said as my fingers brushed across the trigger of my gun.

I was feeling a bit trigger-happy and desperately wanted to empty my clip inside this pussy nigga's skull. Luckily for him, I had a forgiving nature . . . at least for now.

"Now, get the fuck out of here," I threatened while biting my bottom lip as I forcefully pushed him toward the door.

"That's my bad bitch," Beast said as he stood up from his chair.

Turning around, I smiled as my man swaggered over to me. Standing just above six feet, I stared at the fine specimen I considered the sexiest man in the world. With the skin the color of a Hershey's special dark candy bar and a clean-cut with waves so deep that it could make you seasick on sight. All of that is paired with a deep shade of brown eyes, a scar just above one eye, and a perfect white smile. He looked like he should have been a model for Colgate instead of a neighborhood dope boy.

To me, it didn't even matter that he was a bit on the husky side because, although he was fat, his dick was even fatter. The feeling of his hands caressing the sides of my cheeks snapped me out of my thoughts.

"Wassup, daddy?" I purred as his hands traveled down my body and rested between my thighs. As I stared into his eyes, I could feel my juices as they began to flow. My legs shook as he played with my pussy through the thin fabric of my pants. "Hmm," I moaned loudly as I threw my head back in ecstasy while using the table behind me for support.

"Did I tell you to enjoy this shit?" he spat viciously as he wrapped his other hand tightly around my neck.

"N-no," I struggled to answer, but I was still getting turned on at the same time.

"No, what?" he asked as his grip got even tighter.

"No, daddy," I purred as I felt my juices form a puddle in my panties.

"That's a good girl," he replied with a smirk.

Without another word spoken, he spun me around and had me bent over the table. My body slammed into the cold, wooden surface, and within seconds, my pants and panties were ripped off and now rested at my ankles. My sharp, stiletto-styled nails gripped the edge of the table as I stepped out of my pants and panties and kicked them to the side. With one of his hands on my back to keep me in place, my breathing quickened as I braced myself for impact.

"Aah," I moaned out as he began to thrust in and out of me violently.

What was once a puddle was now a river the more he pummeled my pussy. Like I said, we weren't into that mushy lovemaking bullshit. We were into that bruise-making, hardcore fucking. I literally wanted him to fuck me 'til it hurt. Like Sukihana said in one of her lyrics, "fuck my face 'til you bust my lip." That was the kinda shit we were into.

I closed my eyes as I enjoyed the pounding that he was giving my pussy. My man was fucking me so good that

I was starting to see white clouds and the pearly white gates of heaven. To me, his dick was heaven, and I was ready to meet Jesus . . . but upon opening my eyes, it was then that I noticed that Beast's best friend and right-hand man, Bone, was still in the room.

"Get the fuck out of here!" I yelled out in between strokes.

Instead of getting up and leaving like I said, instead, he pulled his dick out of his pants with a smirk plastered across his face as he walked over to us.

"I said," I began before a vicious slap to my right ass cheek caused my words to get caught in my throat.

"And I said shut the fuck up. You're *my* bitch!" he spat. "And if you're my bitch, that means you do whatever I tell you to. Understand?" he asked as he delivered another vicious slap to my ass.

"Yes!" I screamed as I felt my juices squirt out of me and down my legs.

"Now, turn around and face me," he ordered.

With a smirk on my face, I did as I was told. I couldn't help the moans of pleasure that escaped my lips as Beast sucked and bit down on my neck as he sat me back on the table before pushing me down on my back. I never noticed Bone approaching with his erect dick in his hand until he was standing over me. My eyes fluttered as Beast began to finger fuck me.

I was openly willing to give my man whatever he wanted when it came to sex. If he wanted to bring another bitch in the bedroom, I was picking her out. Hell, if he wanted me to eat another bitch's ass while he watched, you could call me Anna Mae because I would eat that cake too. I wasn't a stupid bitch by far, and I knew for a fact that what one woman won't do, a hundred more bitches will. So, I was sure never to leave one stone unturned when it came to my man getting his rocks off.

Preparing for a three-way, I smiled from excitement until Bone walked away from me and went to stand behind Beast. My mouth dropped to the floor when I looked up to see my man dropping his pants and boxers to the floor before bending over the same table that I was lying on.

I now see him getting the same strokes that Beast once delivered to me. To say that I was disgusted by the sight of two men fucking and moaning from each other would have been an understatement, but I knew better than to speak about it. I continued to lie there and watch in horror as my man was getting pounded by another man.

What started out as us fucking, soon turned into them fucking each other without either touching me. I spewed hate as they got up from the table and fixed their clothes. Bone took one last look over his shoulder at me before he walked out the door. It was more than just my man getting fucked by another man that pissed me off. It was how cocky and confident Bone looked at me while he was doing it.

"Now, what the fuck was that?" I yelled as I jumped from the table. "You fucking niggas now? What? My pussy ain't good enough for you?"

Whap!

I immediately fell to the ground as I felt a stinging sensation on the right side of my face. Looking back up, I was no longer looking at the deep shade of brown eyes that I fell in love with so many years ago. I was now looking into a pair of fiery ones as they looked down on me.

"Watch your motherfucking mouth," he threatened.

"What?" I asked sarcastically. "Scared that your little reputation for being a hardcore nigga is gonna be out the window when the rest of these niggas find out that you take it up the ass?"

"You wanna take this up the mouth?"

I once looked into his eyes, but now I was staring down a gun barrel. The same gun that I was aiming at Duke moments ago was now being aimed at me. Being the bitch that I was in these streets and being in the streets like we were, this wasn't the first time that I've had a gun at my head, and I'm sure it wouldn't be the last time either.

Even with me being as crazy as I was and basically knocking on the devil's door with the shit that I was doing, I wasn't trying to get the devil to answer that knock any sooner than he planned. I closed my eyes tightly as I shook my head.

"No."

"Good," he replied, placing the gun back on the table. "Now, get yo' ass up off the floor and go clean yourself."

I bit my bottom lip so hard that it bled as I picked myself up from the floor. It was the only thing I could do to keep me from crying. Some would have thought picking myself up after such a vicious slap would have been harder. Honestly, I had a harder time picking up my ego. For the longest time, I had considered myself *that* bitch in these streets. Unfortunately, I was now *that* bitch who lost her man to another nigga.

Images of Beast getting pounded by Bone kept replaying in my head as I washed myself. They were images that would forever be burned into my memory.

Walking out of the bathroom, I saw Beast sitting at the head of the table with a blunt dangling from his lips. The same lips that I used to love to suck on were just sucking another man's dick. I wanted to throw up at the sight of him, but just like many times before, I kept my composure. I kept my eyes on him as his eyes were trained on me as I walked over to the table and picked up my panties from the floor, but the vision of him and Bone together made me look away. I refused to make eye contact with him. To be honest, I couldn't. I just couldn't bear to face the fact that the man that I loved and would do anything for was into letting men fuck him in the ass.

"You wanna talk about it?" he asked as he exhaled a cloud of smoke.

"Not really."

"You're looking at this as a bad thing," he said as he got up from his seat and walked over to me.

"How else should I look at it?" I asked sarcastically.

"Look at it as a good thing," he answered, holding me by my waist. "Now, I don't have to lie about where I be at late at night when I'm not at home with you. Now, I can just invite Bone over to the house. That way, we can all be together."

"You can't be serious," I stated with wide eyes.

"I'm dead serious. Why can't I be with both of you? Bone has no problem with it. Why should you?"

I couldn't help but look at this nigga as if he had grown two dicks in the middle of his forehead. I guess in his world, two dicks were better than one. The fact that he was saying this shit so calmly was baffling. He was saying it as if he were expecting us to be one big, happy, fucking family. No pun intended on the fucking part.

I couldn't control my eyes twitching as I looked at him. Some would say I was still shocked, while others would say I had just crossed over and into a new level of crazy. Whichever one it was, I was there, and it was because of him. With my man now in the arms of another man, I had nothing else to lose but everything to gain. I just needed to make a plan and follow it.

Chapter Ten

Myleena

I was more than just a little nervous as I walked to class. Although it was always my dream to attend school in America, I never stopped thinking about how different it would be. With Ace walking a few steps behind me, I glanced around as the other students scurried throughout the halls.

I looked up and around as the bell sounded, signaling the beginning of class just as I reached my designated door.

"Aite, Leena," Ace said just as I turned around and faced him. "Go in there and learn something. I'll be waiting for you when you get out," he said with a smile.

I took a deep breath as I gripped the books in my hand. My heart felt like it was racing a mile a minute as I walked through the door. All eyes were on me as I made my way over to the teacher's desk. I felt more like a kid walking in on her first day of elementary school than my first day of college.

"Aah," he said, looking at me as he removed his thick, black-rimmed glasses from his face. "You must be Ms. Myleena Ashik."

"Yes, sir," I answered.

"Well, it's very nice to meet you. My name is Professor Edwards. Go ahead and find yourself a lab group," he instructed.

My heart dropped to the lowest pit of my stomach as I turned around to face the rest of the classroom. The room felt so big, and I felt so small as I walked past each table, where students were already paired in groups of three. It felt like everyone was already situated with their cliques, even with this being only the first day of school. That was until I got to the last table on the right. A girl sat on the end, and a guy wearing a bright pink shirt that read "*That Bitch*" sat right beside her.

"Is this seat taken?" I asked in a voice barely above a whisper.

"Yes," the guy replied while popping his gum. "By you," he said before he broke into a full smile.

I felt relieved for the first time since I stepped foot on campus.

"I'm Dylan," he said, holding out his freshly French-manicured hand at me.

"And I'm Dionne," the girl said.

"I'm Myleena."

"Ooh, I love your accent," Dionne exclaimed. "What are you?"

"Rude much!" Dylan interjected.

"It'll be rude to myself if I didn't ask," she retorted.

"It's okay," I laughed. "I'm slowly but surely getting used to that question, but I'm Indian," I replied.

"Well, it's nice to meet you," Dylan answered before nudging Dionne.

We were interrupted just as I was about to respond.

"Well, it's great that everyone is getting along," Professor Edwards began. "Now, let's get to work. You've all been given a syllabus, and inside that syllabus, you'll see the details for your first group project. You'll all be responsible for your own piece of the project, and I will ask who did which part. The entire group will be penalized if one person doesn't complete the project. Understand?"

"Yes," the class answered in unison.

"All right then," he replied as he glanced around the room. "I want you all to use the rest of your time here to get familiar with each other and what will be expected of you. This is college, not kindergarten. Although I will be here with you, I am not here to hold your hand. That is not how the real world works, so that's not how my class will work either. The group you're with now will remain your group for the rest of the semester unless I feel changes should be made."

We continued to get to know each other as Dylan basically took charge of when we would be doing what within the group.

"All right, so with us only having about a week to get this project done, I suggest we get started on it today," he said as he looked between Dionne and me.

"Why not just wait until the day before it's due," Dionne suggested as she turned her gaze to Dylan.

"And that's exactly why this is your third time taking this course," he answered with a giggle.

His comment made my eyes bulge, and my mouth hit the table as I stared at Dionne.

"What do you think, Myleena?" they asked.

"Do you want to start now? That way, we can perfect it and get a good grade. Or do you want to wait until the last minute like Ms. Dionne just suggested and possibly flunk the rest of this class?"

"I don't want to fail," I replied.

"Great," Dylan said as he snapped his fingers in Dionne's face before laughing. "That solves it. Now, we'll meet this afternoon at your place," he said to me.

"Wait, what?"

"Yeah. Why not?" he asked rhetorically.

"Why my place?" I asked as I looked at them.

"Well, unfortunately, my apartment is being renovated, and Dionne lives in the projects. There's no way I'll be stepping foot in that place again. Them bitches will steal the panties right off your ass and then help you look for them."

"Bitch, you overexaggerating like a motherfucker," Dionne exclaimed.

"Oh, I'm exaggerating?" Dylan asked sarcastically. "What about the time I spent the night over yo' place, and I lost my neon pink G-strings, and that bitch Angie came over the next day wearing them?"

I couldn't help but burst into laughter at them as they continued to go back and forth. Looking around the classroom, I noticed that all eyes were on them. I would have thought that with them being the center of attention, they would have calmed down, but I was wrong. And I thought their little outburst would have made the teacher tell them to quiet down, but he said nothing. It looked as if he were just as interested in their conversation as the rest of the class.

"Well, she offered to give them back," Dionne said through her laughter.

"Do you *really* think that I would accept them panties after she wore them? Wear panties after the same bitch who's at the free clinic twice a week? After the same bitch that got green shit coming outta her pussy and got the nerve to say that it's *normal?* Bitch, you *ain't* normal," he said while shaking his head.

"Bitch, I cannot," Dionne laughed. "I cannot!"

"No, bitch. *I* cannot," he replied. "Now, back to the matter at hand. Your place today around four?"

"Umm, okay," I replied with a sweet smile.

"All right then, it's settled. Here's my number," he said as he wrote it down on a sheet of paper.

"And here's mines," Dionne stated. "Just text me your address."

"What you need the address for? You don't even have a car. Whatchu gonna do, use yo' GPS and skate over there? Girl, please," he said as he sucked his teeth.

Before I could say anything else, the bell rang again, and everyone jumped up from their seats and practically ran for the door. I took a deep breath as I stood up from my seat.

"Enjoy the rest of your day, Ms. Ashik," Mr. Edwards said with a smile.

"Thank you," I replied.

Thankfully, the rest of the day flew by, and thankfully, Nitro was okay with Dionne and Dylan coming over to work on our project for school. I was happy when Ace and I finally walked to the parking lot and got into the car. I thought of Nitro as Ace weaved in and out of traffic on the highway. Just the thought of Nitro made me smile. I'm sure that my father would smack me into the ground and threaten to cut off my head if he knew of my thoughts about him, but while it was a sin for my thoughts, I couldn't ignore the connection that I felt toward him whenever he was around or the things that I would willingly do for him.

When he had a bad day, I was always there with a joke to make him smile, even if they were what he would consider to be corny. When I could see that he would have a long day at work, I was always sure to ask him if there was anything I could do to help. Since I knew that LaToya wasn't big on cooking, whenever I cooked for myself, I would always make extra to ensure that he never went to bed hungry. I knew that LaToya was his woman, so I was sure never to overstep my boundaries and never speak about the fact that I never went to bed without ensuring he had arrived home safely.

There were times when I would catch myself daydreaming about what and how my life would be if Nitro and I were together, but just as quickly as those thoughts would enter my mind, they were out just as fast. LaToya was never subtle about her title of being Nitro's woman. She had no problem throwing it in my face when I offered to do the simplest things for him, things like taking his dishes to the sink after he finished eating. Something that was a regular chore for me in my country was a sign of disrespect to LaToya in this country.

"Hey, Leena. You still in there?" Ace asked as he waved his hand in front of my face.

"Yeah," I chuckled while shaking my head in embarrassment.

"We're here," he announced.

Looking out the window, I smiled as we now sat in front of Nitro's home. I quickly reached for the handle and walked up the stone pathway until I reached the door. To my dismay, as soon as I walked in, I saw LaToya sitting in the living room, flipping through the channels on the television. She didn't bother speaking to me as I entered. Instead, she just sucked her teeth and rolled her eyes before turning her attention back to the television.

"Hey, LaToya," I said as I passed by her.

"Hmm," was all that she said as I walked to my room.

Just as I was at my door, I bumped into Nitro. I looked up and stared into his dark brown eyes as he stared into my gray ones. A contagious smile appeared on his face, which caused one to spread to mine, a smile that was starting to happen more often whenever he was around.

"How was school?" he asked.

"It was good," I answered shyly.

That familiar yet weird feeling came back. The feeling that I only got when he was around. The feeling of a million and one butterflies flapping around in my stomach. The feeling of my heart as if it were about to beat out of my chest. Although I was looking at him speaking, I couldn't hear what he was saying for some reason.

"I heard it was better than good," he commented.

"What?"

"I hear that you made some friends."

"Umm, I guess so. It's only for a school project. It's still okay if they come over, right?" I asked.

"Why wouldn't it be?"

"Umm, I see that LaToya is in the living room. I didn't want to intrude on her or anything."

"Don't worry about that," he assured me with another dazzling smile. "She ain't doing nothing and wasn't even in there until I told her that you was having company."

"Oh," I answered as I looked toward the living room and then back to Nitro. "Well, I'll be in my room if you need me," I replied before scurrying away.

I quickly looked around to make sure that it was suitable for company. Taking off my shoes, I placed my sneakers into the box and put the box under the bed. Some of my customs have changed since I've been in this country. Since Nitro is such a neat freak, and LaToya looks for any reason to start an argument, I always kept it clean. Not to mention, Nitro practically had a twenty-four-hour maid. If it were up to him, I would never even have to make my own bed, but I was determined to do as much for myself as possible. I was tired of living the life of the pampered and privileged. After tidying up, I sat on the floor and enjoyed the softness of the area rug.

"Hello, Ms. Myleena."

Looking up, I smiled at Mrs. Valdez. She was Nitro's housekeeper, and just like Ace, she couldn't stand LaToya and never tried to hide it. In fact, she made her disdain for LaToya as clear as day and always turned up her nose at her whenever she was around.

"Hello, Mrs. Valdez. How are you?" I asked as I got up from the floor.

She was actually a very beautiful woman. She closely resembled an older version of Gabby from *Desperate Housewives,* a show that I was becoming fond of.

"I'm doing fine. Thanks for asking. Is there anything that I can do for you? I've heard that you're having a study party. How about I whip up some snacks for you and your guests?"

"I don't want to put you to any trouble."

"No trouble at all," she replied with a smile. "I'd rather do this for you than that lazy, noncooking *punta,* LaToya," she said with her thick Hispanic accent.

I couldn't help but giggle. She spoke the words on everyone's lips who had ever met LaToya.

"Thank you."

"No problem at all. Just the thought of that psycho makes me want to drink," she spat as she walked away, talking more in her own language.

Just as Mrs. Valdez left, the doorbell rang. My heart raced as I practically jogged down the steps toward the front door. My dad never allowed my sisters or me to have company, so this was a first, and while I was nervous, I was also excited.

Chapter Eleven

Dionne

"Damn," I exclaimed as Dylan and I pulled up to the address that Myleena sent to us.

For some reason, I was expecting to pull up to a plain old house on a street in a common area of the city. I never expected us to be directed to one of the most expensive and exclusive parts of the city. We made multiple turns throughout the neighborhood until we drove down a long and narrow road. That road soon led to a beautiful house resembling a mini-mansion to me.

When our eyes landed on the place, our mouths damn near hit the floor of Dylan's hooptie.

"Damn," I exclaimed again. "I knew the bitch was getting money. But by no means was I thinking was she *this* paid."

"What makes you think that she's paid?" Dylan asked as he looked back at me from the house.

"Dylan, don't sit here and act like you didn't notice that nigga waiting outside of the classroom door. Not to mention him pulling up the car and shit. This bitch has a bodyguard and personal chauffeur all wrapped into one. She's *definitely* getting money."

"There you go, always assuming shit. That could be her big brother, for all you know."

"Whatever, Dylan. I *know* what the fuck I'm talking about," I spat as I rolled my eyes at him.

"Whatever. You just behave," he replied with a smack of his lips before getting out of the car with his purse and other bags in his hand.

Together, we walked up the stone walkway to the magnificent home. Just the front yard of this house was the size of my entire apartment. We looked at each other before we rang the doorbell. Moments later, the door swung open, and we were greeted by a beautiful woman with the ugliest scowl.

A few seconds passed with us staring at one another before Dylan finally opened his mouth to speak.

"Hey, my name is Dylan, and this is Dionne. We're here for Myleena," he said as he greeted the woman. "We're here for our study party," he said as he did a little dance.

"I know who you are and why you're here," she spat with a roll of her eyes. "Come on in."

Dylan stared at this broad like she was crazy for how she was coming at us. Bitch didn't even know us but was already coming outta her neck sideways. I balled up my fist and looked down at my sneakers, making sure that they were tied up tight because I just knew I was about stomp this bitch out of her Maybelline and through the floor. Sensing my attitude about to flare up, Dylan looked at me with eyes that told me to chill. Knowing that I couldn't get another charge on my record, I counted back from ten before finally regaining my composure.

Although she ushered us in with her words, her vibe and tone screamed the complete opposite. But we followed her into the house anyway. From the vibes that I was getting from shawty, I was sure to keep an eye on this bitch for as long as she was in my presence . . . and even after. Eyes like that only told me that this bitch couldn't be trusted and that she would possibly sneak my ass if she got the opportunity.

Upon stepping inside the house, we were utterly blown away. If the outside of the house were jaw-dropping, the inside of it would have made you shit bricks. The inside looked completely presidential and so expensive it felt like it would break if you looked at it too hard.

"I told you this bitch was paid," I whispered to Dylan as we continued to follow the woman.

While glancing at us over her shoulder, she led us into a living that could have easily sat a classroom full of people. It was then that Myleena finally made her grand entrance. One thing about me was that I paid attention to everything, and I noticed that whoever this woman was, she was definitely not a fan of Myleena's.

After a brief stare down between the two, the woman who opened the door for us finally walked out of the room.

"I'm sorry about that. That was LaToya. She's the girlfriend of the guy I'm staying with," she told us.

"Wait, what?" I asked, being nosy. "You're staying with a man who has a girlfriend? Why?"

"Umm . . ." she said as she nervously looked around. "That's a long story."

"Don't worry about it. We have nothing but time." I responded.

"Myleena, don't worry about Dionne. She just don't know when to stop," Dylan replied as he slapped me on my arm. "Don't worry. After a while, you'll learn to ignore her. I have."

"Thanks," she replied nervously.

From the look on her face, I could tell that my line of questioning was making her uncomfortable, but if we were going to be friends, it was time for her to learn what kind of bitch I was. I was the kind of bitch who asked and said whatever was on my mind. I mean, how else were we gonna get to know one another if I didn't ask questions? Just as much as I was curious about her life, I made a note in the back of my head to ask her again, but later on in the future.

"So, let's crack open these books and get to work," Dylan said as he clapped his hands together and sat on the sectional.

Myleena couldn't help but laugh, which, in turn, caused me to laugh too. Dylan and I had been friends since middle school, so I was used to his antics and flamboyant ways. It was actually one of the reasons that I loved him. Back where we used to live, or rather, where I *still* lived, it was hard to be out of the closet without people looking at you funny, but not me. I welcomed it. Like me, Dylan wasn't afraid of being the true him out in the open. That was actually one of his greatest qualities. He lived a life that wasn't easy, and that alone made him a lot easier to talk to because, no matter what, he never judged. At the end of the day, that's all anybody wants . . . not to be judged for who they are.

We all grabbed our supplies and took a spot on the floor. Dylan read out the plans he had drawn up, and Myleena and I followed by making a design on the chart.

"Use more colors, bitch," Dylan said to me. "I want our shit to pop. I want our shit to be seen a mile away," he ordered.

"And just like those bright-ass pants you got on. Those colors are fucking with my eyes," I complained while still doing what he said.

"That's why you would never make it as a gay bitch. You see, we like to be seen, not just heard. We damn sure don't like to play the background," he said with a pop of his tongue.

"Whatever," I laughed while adding more colors to the board.

Looking over, I saw Myleena's eyes as she stared at Dylan.

"You good?" I asked.

"Yeah," she replied, shaking her head and getting back to the paper. It wasn't before long that I noticed her staring at Dylan again, only this time, he was looking back.

"What's wrong, girl?" he asked. "Is my lip gloss smearing?"

"Oh no. I just . . . I just," she stuttered.

"You just what?" we both asked.

And although she was staring at him, I was the one getting defensive. As I said, a lot of people didn't accept Dylan's way of living and considered him to be an abomination in the eyes of God. With him basically being my sister from another mister, I was always down to throw down in the name of him. He was a female at heart, although his identification card still said male. So, I would never allow him to beat a bitch. That was always my job, and this time would be no different.

"I've never met anyone who was gay before," she confessed. "Actually, I never met anyone before other than the people my father hired to protect me."

"Protect you?" I asked.

"Yeah," she said as tears soon appeared in her eyes.

"Protect you from what?"

"I guess I might as well tell you." She took a deep breath before she began to speak. Dylan and I sat there motionless as she told us everything. Everything from why she was here to what had happened to her family back in her country. As the tears fell, Dylan and I rushed to her side to comfort her. As we listened to her silently cry, I couldn't help but think about my own family. Although they irritated me to the point of drinking rubbing alcohol, I don't know what I would do if anything were to ever happen to any of them.

"Well, we're family now," Dylan said. "We got yo' back."

We all laughed as Myleena sniffled back her tears. Dylan and I could both see that talking was making her feel better as she began to laugh too.

"Well, now that y'all know, let's get back to work," she said.

The front door soon opened, followed by a set of heavy footsteps. A fresh pair of Tims stood in the middle of the doorway. Looking up, my eyes landed on the sexiest man that I had ever seen. A man who was so sexy that he would give Michael Ealy a run for his money. He had dreads that hung to his shoulders with light brown tips and a set of deep, dark brown eyes. Some would call seeing him love at first sight. Upon further examination, I realized that it was none other than the guy who had been escorting Myleena to and from school.

"Hey, Ace," Myleena said with a small smile.

My heart dropped to the lowest pit of my stomach at the smile that crossed Myleena's face as she looked at the man.

"Hey," he replied. "Where's Nitro?" he asked as he looked from me to Dylan. "Hey," he said to us.

"Hey," Dylan and I both sang.

I looked over at Dylan. He was smiling like the cat who got the canary.

"He's in his office," Myleena answered.

Just as she spoke, a pair of Adidas sneakers entered the room. I gazed up and over at Myleena and saw an even bigger smile plastered on her face as she looked at the handsome stranger. It was as if time stood still as the two locked eyes on each other. Wondering if I was the only one catching on to their electric connection, I looked at Dylan and could only shake my head. He looked like a lovesick teenager with his first crush. Looking at Dylan as he looked at the two men, it was as if he were about to have a heart attack and go straight to rainbow heaven, probably thinking of all the ways that he could be flipping this man's ass around. I nudged him as he was practically drooling at the sight of the men.

"Get back to work and stop staring so damn hard," I whispered harshly.

"Whatever," he replied before smacking his lips together again.

After taking one last look at us, the two men excused themselves and walked to the back of the house. We all waited until we heard the door close before we tore into Myleena's ass.

"Who the hell were they?" I was the first to ask. "The dude with the fade is cute, but the nigga with the dreads is *everything,*" I practically screamed, almost having an orgasm just from the sight of him.

"That's Ace."

"Yeah. I heard that part, but who is he?" I asked, ready to get down to the bottom of it. "And most importantly, is he single? 'Cause if so, I'ma need you to hook that up."

"That's Nitro's best friend, and I'm not sure if he's single, but I'll ask."

"And Nitro is?" Dylan asked.

"That's the guy I'm staying with," she blushed.

"And the guy who also already has a woman."

Turning around, we once again saw the woman whose ass I was about to drag if it weren't for Dylan. I looked at her as she looked down at us, but more so at Myleena. If eyes could shoot daggers, Myleena's ass would have been hanging like a picture, but as Dylan said, we were family now, and I was prepared to throw hands for her too, if it came down to it.

"I know that," Myleena replied.

"Okay," she replied with a fake smile. "Don't forget it. Have a nice study party," she said sarcastically as she walked down the hallway and out the door.

I rolled my eyes at her before turning back to Myleena.

"That bitch is gonna be the reason I catch another charge," I spat with venom. "What's up with her?"

"I don't know. She's never liked me."

"Shit, if I had a man that looked as good as him, I wouldn't like yo' ass either," Dylan laughed. "That man is *fine*."

"Fuck that stank ho. What I wanna know is, what's up with you and him?"

"What?" she asked as the color drained from her face. "What are you talking about?"

"That bitch might be stank, but just like me, she has eyes. You and Nitro have some kinda attraction to each other."

"Oh no. I could never," she said as she repeatedly shook her head.

"Yes, you could," I assured her. "Like you told us, you're not in your country anymore. You can be whatever kind of woman that you want."

"I wouldn't even know what to do," she replied slowly.

"That's what you got me for," Dylan said. "Besides, I don't like that bitch. So, I'm gonna help you get this nigga so that bitch can be nothing but a bad memory."

Chapter Twelve

Nitro

"Since when do you let people you don't know come to yo' house?" Ace questioned as soon as the door to my office was closed.

"Shit, what else can I do? It's for her class," I replied, shrugging my shoulders. "Best believe I'm watching they asses."

"I bet. I can see that LaToya ain't too fond of that decision."

"When is LaToya ever fond of anything that ain't gonna benefit her?" I asked sarcastically.

"That's yo' girl."

"I guess so," I replied.

"So, what's the word on that new connect?" Ace asked as I took a seat in my chair, and he sat across from me.

"He seems legit, and the product seems pure. Not to mention, a few stacks cheaper than what we paying with Pablo."

"Is that right?" he asked as he perked up in his chair. "So, what you telling me is that it might be time to cut our ties with Pablo?" he asked.

"I wouldn't do it just yet. I'm still trying to feel out this new nigga. Can't throw in our hand until we know it's a for-sure win."

"I gotchu. Anything you need me to do?"

"Nah," I said as I shook my head. "Just keep watching out for Myleena when I'm not around. I can take care of everything else."

"Gotcha, but in other news, there's some new niggas on the block who are trying to take over our turfs."

"I know," I replied.

"You know?" Ace asked in a surprised tone. "And you not doing anything about it?"

"Not until I know who they getting their supply from."

"But they're selling their shit at dirt-cheap prices. At the rate they're going, they gonna take our customers."

"That's a risk that I'm willing to take. They might be able to take our customers, but will they be able to keep them? That's the bigger question. Selling product cheap is a good idea to attract customers, but to keep the customers, they'll have to keep those same prices or have the purest shit out there in order to raise their prices. Since we have the purest shit, they'll either have to buy from us or lose to us. My guess is that them niggas are gonna dig themselves into a hole so deep that they won't be able to get out. So, either way, we win."

I smirked at Ace as he nodded his head in agreement. My father always taught me to look at every situation and evaluate it until you know all possible outcomes. Like I said, there was little to nothing that went on in these streets that I didn't know about.

"If you give a nigga enough rope, they'll eventually hang themselves. Them new niggas ain't no exception, but just in case, get Steele and Monster to sit on them niggas."

"Say less," Ace replied, getting up from the chair with his phone in hand. That was one thing I liked about Ace.

He wasn't a wait-and-see type of nigga. He was all about action and always ready to put in work.

I sat back and stared at the ceiling as I thought about my next move. With my dad about to hand me the empire he built from the ground up, I was more determined than I ever have been. I wanted to show him that he had made the right decision to make me his successor. Grabbing my keys off the desk, I passed by Ace as he spoke on the phone.

"I'm heading out," I called out over my shoulder. "Once they gone, lock up. I'll meet you at the spot in the morning."

"Done," he replied before going back to his call.

All eyes were on me as I walked through the living room. Stopping, I looked down at Myleena, who was focused on whatever book she was reading. It wasn't until her friend cleared her throat that she looked up at me. Damn, there was something about them eyes that made my heart go soft.

"Did you need something?" she asked with a look of worry.

"Nah, I was just heading out. I wanted to see if you needed anything."

"No. I'm okay. Thank you," she replied with a shy smile.

If her eyes were hypnotizing, then her smile was definitely putting my ass in a trance. I had to get up out of there before I said something stupid. Nodding my head to her friends, I said my goodbyes and walked out. I had a few errands to run before nightfall.

Getting in my car, I let the sunroof back and allowed the sun to shine through. My cream leather interior looked good to the eye but felt even better. I sparked a blunt as I put the key in the ignition before pulling out of the driveway. Kevin Gates spilled through my speakers as I drove down the narrow road that led to the rest of the neighborhood. One thing about me was that I liked privacy. You had to make many turns to get to my front door. If anyone was able to find it, they either knew me personally or they were shot on sight.

I was barely five minutes from the house before my phone alerted me to text messages. A feeling of irritation rested in my chest at the sight of LaToya's name flashing across the screen. It felt like she would always find a reason to complain no matter what. It's true, I never allowed people that I didn't know come to or even to know where I rested my head, but at the end of the day, this was a safe place for Myleena, and that was my job: to keep her safe. So, come hell or high water, that's what I was gonna do.

Not to mention, I already had a good friend do their research on her two friends. I knew everything from where they stayed all the way down to their jobs and family homes. If they became a problem to me, I would become a permanent solution to them.

Instead of replying to any of her many messages, I simply placed my phone in the cup holder. I had more pressing matters to deal with than her jealous ass. After driving about twenty minutes through what would be considered the worst neighborhood in New York, I arrived at my destination. I checked my waist to ensure that my gun was there and that it was off safety. No matter how big of a deal I was in the streets, I knew that there were always niggas who wanted my spot. To ensure that taking my spot wouldn't be easy, I was always sure to be my own protection and to treat every transaction like a life-or-death situation because, at the end of the day, that's precisely what it was. At any given time, my life could be taken, all for the almighty dollar.

I nodded at the corner boys as I walked up the crack-infested sidewalk. With one hand holding a black duffle bag and the other hand brandishing my gun, I opened the door to the raggedy apartment complex. Crackheads and the smell of piss greeted me upon entry. I stepped over the people as they lay sprawled out on the floor, and then I walked up the stairs.

"Aye, my brother," a man said as he stepped from a dark corner. "You got anything to spare?" he asked with a needle still poking out of his arm.

"Naw, brother. I'm afraid not. I'm sure them brothers out there got plenty. Go see 'bout that."

"Them niggas ain't got shit, but I see ya," he replied as he walked away from me and down the stairs with the rest of the fiends.

I knocked twice on the last door on the right side, and within seconds, I heard locks being slid and chains being unfastened before the door swung open.

"Wassup, Bear?" I greeted as I walked in. "How's business going?"

I looked at a man I knew back when I first started out. The reason the streets called him Bear was because if you walked up to him, you would think that this nigga was an actual bear. From his big frame to how hairy the nigga's face was, it was a name that definitely fit his description.

"Better than ever. There are a few slipups, but nothing I can't handle. What about you?" he asked as he grabbed the duffel bag. "How's life?"

"Life is good. I'm just tryin'a eat," I replied.

"Well, let me holla at you about that," he said as he sat at a wooden kitchen table.

Following suit, I sat across from him. Just as he was about to speak, a thick redbone appeared from one of the back rooms. She wore a black lace robe and walked through the kitchen like we weren't even there. She kind of put me in the mind of a young LisaRaye, back when she played as Diamond on *The Players Club*.

"Wassup?" I asked Bear.

"Do you want something to drink?" shawty asked flirtatiously as she looked at me.

"Nah, I'm good," I answered.

"Are you sure?" she asked again. "I can give you anything you want," she said as she bent slightly over, trying to expose her cleavage, but I was instantly turned off by the track marks in the crease of her arm.

"Angie, what the fuck is that?" Bear asked as he looked at the woman with narrow eyes. "Why you all in that man face for?"

"Bear, you tripping," she said as she put her hands on her thick hips. "I'm just trying to take care of him. The same I do with all the niggas that work here."

"This man don't work here. He *own* this shit. He own *you*," he stated.

"That's all more of a reason to take care of him," she said with a smile as she turned her attention back to me.

"Nah, I'm good."

"Well, you be sure to let me know if there's anything you need," she said as she swished her way down the hall. "Anything," she threw over her shoulder before she closed the bedroom door behind her.

"My bad about that. That bitch just don't know how to act like a lady, but I guess that's something that can't be taught or bought," he said with a laugh.

"No problem at all. Now, let's get back to what you wanted to discuss."

"A'ight. So, check it; there's some new cats on the block that's trying to sell."

"Okay."

"And with me being me, I know there's enough money out here for everybody to eat. We just gotta do it the right way."

"And?" I said, waiting for him to get right to the point.

"So, I pulled the nigga to the side that they said was in charge. You know, kinda to put a bug in his ear. I told him that if he want to eat, he gotta pull up a seat to the table."

"And what did he say?"

"He said fuck our table. He said he's gonna build and eat at his own table," he answered as veins began to pop out his forehead.

"So, what you thinking?"

"I'm thinking that this nigga want a fucking war, and I'll give him one before I lose the way I eat and feed my family."

"Won't be necessary, believe it or not, but I'm already aware of this situation, and I'ma just let it play out. Stay cool until further notice. Since that nigga wanna build his own table, if he jump crooked, you have my permission to serve him his last meal. Other than that, I'ma let these niggas run themselves into the ground."

"I feel you, boss man."

We spoke on a few more business matters before I made my way back out the door and to my car. Once I got in my car, I checked my phone and wasn't surprised to see that I had over twenty missed calls from LaToya, including sixteen voicemails. Already knowing what kind of mood she was probably in, I decided against returning any of her messages. Instead, I finished the blunt I started and continued on with the rest of my errands.

Before long, it was nightfall, and I finished with my runs and was heading back home. I was beyond tired and ready to call it a night. I was even more thankful that it was a Saturday night, which meant tonight was the night that LaToya was working the night shift. Although that still did not affect her blowing up my phone, it gave me relief knowing that I wouldn't have to deal with her ass in person. At least not tonight.

The ride home was quick and quiet as I placed my keys on the table in the hallway. A smirk appeared on my face after seeing the shadow of Myleena as she walked down the hallway, which led to her room before I heard the door close behind her. Walking into the kitchen, my smirk turned into a full smile at seeing a plate sitting on the kitchen table for me. Something that was beginning to turn into a routine for her. Walking over to it, I was pleased to see it was still hot.

Removing the wrap, the smell of the food immediately made my stomach growl. I don't know what the hell I was eating, but it was better than anything I've ever tasted. I could have been eating a dog, for all I know. I guess with the right seasonings, I could eat anything that she made. Ten minutes later, I was licking my fingers and burping from the well-cooked meal.

I smiled at the thought of Myleena. In so many ways, she was different from LaToya. Where LaToya was known for always ordering out, Myleena was famous for always being in the kitchen. Where my mother couldn't stand LaToya, my mother completely adored Myleena, which was a challenging task since my mother barely liked anyone.

Damn, I thought as I lay in bed and looked at the ceiling. *If only our worlds weren't so different. She probably could have been the one.* Thoughts of Myleena sleeping next to me were the last thoughts to cross my mind before I closed my eyes and drifted off to sleep.

Chapter Thirteen

LaToya

I huffed and puffed like a scolded child as I sat at the nurse's station and watched reruns of episodes of *Love* and *Hip-Hop*. Occasionally, I would glance down the hallway to ensure that none of my residents were out of bed and wandering the halls. To say that I had an attitude would have been an understatement. I was in no mood to be in here taking care of these old motherfuckers who saw nursing assistants as nothing more than indentured servants instead of as people. It didn't matter that the shift was easy and the work was even easier. I would have rather been at Nitro's place with him blowing out my back.

Just thinking about my man and that third leg that he called a dick caused chills to shoot down my spine. It should've been a crime for a man to do the things that he was able to do to a woman's body. Which is why I wasn't thrilled at all with having my man share his space with another woman other than me. That bitch thought that I couldn't see what she was trying to do. As I said before, my vision may not have been all that clear, but when it came to my man and securing my meal ticket, my vision would go from twenty/ten to twenty/twenty in a heartbeat.

Nitro may not have been able to see what she was trying to do, but I did. I was once in her shoes too, plotting and scheming how to secure the future king of New York in my bed and in my purse. It may have taken a few fistfights, calls to other bitches to tell them that he was mine, faking a few pregnancies, and even me losing my best friend since the first grade to get him, but I did. To me, that was all that mattered.

Most would say that I was wrong for what I've done to secure my place as number one in Nitro's life. But the way I saw it was, friendship wasn't going to keep me out of the welfare line, and it damn sure wasn't going to buy me the Louis Vuitton purses and diamond rings that I felt like I deserved. Shit, Ronnie wasn't lying when she said that sometimes you gotta use what you got to get what you want. God saw fit to bless me with a phat ass, a curvy frame, plump titties, and a thick set of lips, and I planned to use them all to my benefit.

I refused to end up like my mother, an old and bitter bitch who had nothing better to do than sit on her raggedy-ass stoop in the hood and talk about everybody else. Nah, I had bigger and better plans for *my* life. Now, don't get me wrong. My mother used to be a very beautiful woman. She's where I got my looks from. But unlike her, I had a better and stronger mind frame than her. I wasn't going to use my looks to earn me a date, a wet ass, and a few dollars from a baller. Hell no. I was using mine to set me up for life, and that's where Nitro came in.

Nitro has always been a well-known hustler throughout the hood. Now, word on the streets is that his father was about to retire from the game, and guess who was gonna be running shit after Willie left? That's right. Nitro. So, the way I saw it, I was a smart bitch to play my part as his bitch because, in due time, I was going to be "*That* Bitch.*"

A smile crossed my plush lips as I thought about the life I would soon be living. The life of a kingpin's bitch . . . the life of the rich. Soon, I would be able to leave this god-forsaken job, leave my tiny apartment, and move into a more luxurious place with Nitro. All I had to do was get this terroristic-looking bitch and his mother out of the way, tie up a few loose ends, and all would be right with the world.

Looking down the hall, my eyes wandered over to the sitting area. I instantly got irritated as Naomi had her lunch with Joe. Here it was, eleven o'clock at night, and these two motherfuckers were all lovey-dovey in the dining area, feeding each other chocolate-covered strawberries and shit. I couldn't help but roll my eyes at them. Although they were voted the Couple of the Year at the job, just seeing them made me sick.

I shook my head as I tried to rid myself of my irritated thoughts and focus back on *Love* and *Hip-Hop*. Although they were old episodes, they were the episodes that I enjoyed the most. Episodes that didn't seem as scripted as they are now.

I laughed hysterically at how crazy in love Tommie was with Scrapp DeLeon. One minute the bitch was mad and unimpressed that he stopped by, and the next minute, she was crying because he was about to dip. That bitch was straight up lock-me-in-a-strait-jacket-and-throw-away-the-key type of crazy, but in a weird way, I completely understood how she felt. All because they were feelings that I shared about Nitro.

Our relationship was far from perfect. Sometimes, he would piss me off to the max, but as soon as he threatened to leave, my walls, which I thought were so strong, would come crumbling down. Nitro was my soft spot, the love of my wallet, my drug of choice. I would kill the president to keep him.

Looking down the hall, I couldn't help but roll my eyes again. This time, it was at the light at the end of the hall, signaling that a resident needed help with something. Gazing back over to the dining area at Naomi and Joe, I could see that the light didn't concern them. They were too busy swapping spit and sucking tongues. Pushing myself away from the desk, I walked down the hall toward the light while peeking inside each room, just so the cameras could see that I was doing my hourly rounds.

"Yes, Mrs. Parker," I said as I opened the door. "Do you need something?"

The smell of shit filled the air and smacked me right in the face as I stood in the doorway. The smell instantly made me gag and regret coming to answer this light. As a matter of fact, Mrs. Parker was considered to be one of Naomi's residents for the night.

"Can you not smell what the fuck I need help with?" she spat with attitude. "Get your ass over here and get me to the bathroom."

"*Excuse* me?" I asked as my eyebrows shot up in surprise.

"You heard me. Get over here and clean me up. Or do you not like your job?" she said as she struggled to put her dentures into her mouth.

This bitch had some fucking nerve talking to me like that. Here she was, the one needing my help to wipe her ass, but she was talking to me like I was asking her for change on the street. Instead of laying her ass out like I wanted to, I politely smiled and walked back toward the nursing station. Just as I reached the dining area, I saw Naomi and Joe as they were locking lips again.

"Aye, Naomi. I can see you're having a grand time swapping spit with Joe, but Mrs. Parker needs to be changed."

"Can you do it?" she asked in between kisses. "I'm a little busy at the moment."

"No. Technically, she's your resident," I replied. "And you might want to hurry. She looks like she's getting impatient, and we both know she'll try to take herself to the bathroom. I doubt you want to have to fill out any incident reports or check her vitals every fifteen minutes for the rest of your shift," I said as I looked from her to Joe. "I'm sure that'll ruin the plans you've made."

She sucked her teeth as I walked away with the most sinister smile on my face. That bitch thought that she was gonna have an easy night. Well, think again, bitch. I was the type of bitch where if I wasn't having a good night, no one else would either. What better way to begin your night than to clean up some shit.

I walked back to my chair and immediately grabbed my phone. I was surprised and a bit upset that Nitro hadn't called or texted to check on me all the time that I was gone. Looking at the clock on the wall, I knew that it was always around this time that Nitro would be arriving home. One thing I loved about him was that it didn't matter what happened in the streets. He always made it home at around the same time.

"Two hours down, ten more to go," I said as I got comfortable in my chair.

Chapter Fourteen

Dionne

(Three Days Later)

"A'ight, bitch," Dylan shouted through his car window as I walked through the courtyard that led to my apartment building. "I'll see you tomorrow. Bitch, this time, you better be ready on time. If yo' ass is even one minute late, yo' ass will be pounding the pavement to class. Believe me, this heat and yo' edges don't mix."

I shook my head and laughed as his ass burned rubber out of the parking lot. His ass meant what he said when he said that he would rather die a straight man before stepping foot back into Vinegar Hill Housing Projects. True to his word, neither his Louis Vuitton sneakers nor his size eleven Red Bottoms stilettos ever stepped foot back into these apartments. The most that he would do is sit in his 2002 Honda with the doors locked and wait for me to come to him.

It didn't matter that he used to live here before his sugar daddy bought him a condo on the Upper East Side of Manhattan. As crazy as he talked, he wasn't lying when he said that bitches here would steal yo' shit and then help you look for it. It had been done to me plenty of times. As bad as I wanted to leave these projects, I couldn't. It was my home. My mother lived one floor above me, and my sister lived beside me. Not to mention, a few of my cousins also lived in the same building as me. And we were always over at one another's houses. So, it actually felt like we lived in a big-ass mansion.

As soon as I walked into the apartment building, the pungent stench of urine smacked me in the face. Some would call it disgusting, but like I said, it was home.

"Wassup, Dionne?" My cousin Cali said to me as I walked up the stairs.

"Hey."

"How was school?"

"It was all right," I answered.

"Had to have been more than all right," my other cousin Angie interrupted as she walked toward me. "I see yo' little friend Dylan still scared to bring his prissy ass farther than the parking lot. What, he scared someone gonna try to steal his boy pussy?"

"Scared of stealing his boy pussy? No," I answered rhetorically. "But you the bitch that stole his G-strings."

"I didn't steal shit. I saw a brand-new pair of panties on the floor. They were cute and my size, so I took them. Speaking of which, I'm wearing them right now," she bragged as she turned around, giving us a full view of the crack of her ass. "Besides, what the fuck was he doing with them anyways?"

"Apparently, the same thing you did with them," I yelled. "Wear them. I mean, what kinda ho would steal another woman's, or in better words, another man's piss catchers? Like, what kinda shit is that?"

I could feel myself growing impatient the more that I talked to her. Angie was a different kind of bitch. Shit, truth be told, if she weren't family, I probably would've dusted off this ho. Ever since we were young, she always thought that since she was a high-yellow, redbone bitch she could do and say whatever she pleased. For a while, she got away with it. Little did she know, the shit was getting really old and really fast. If she didn't watch who she was talking to, she would eventually learn that bitches around these parts didn't give a fuck about complexion. In fact, they'd stomp her ass out just because she was light skinned.

"Whatever, ho," she spat back. "His ass didn't need 'em no way. Where was he gonna put his dick at anyway?" she asked smartly as she popped her gum and twirled her dry tracks with her fingers.

"He can tuck it behind his ass and pretend it's a tail for all I care. If that's what he wanna do, so be it. You just be sure to keep yo' thieving ass away from my door," I yelled back as I slammed the door in her face.

I dropped my bags at the door and immediately kicked off my shoes. Dump or not, I was glad to be home. Today was a long day, but thankfully, it was over, and we got a good grade on our first project for the semester. I smiled as I thought of how Dylan was smiling and bragging, saying we got a good grade because of his directions. I swear, he was the most irritating person when he was right, but at the same time, I don't know what I would do without him.

I grabbed a pint of Rocky Road ice cream from the freezer and went to my bedroom. With my spoon dangling from my mouth, I plopped down on my bed and turned on the television. I flicked through a few channels before turning it off because nothing interesting was on. Grabbing my phone, I scrolled through Facebook and smiled. It hadn't even been an hour since Dylan dropped me off, and he was already with his sugar daddy.

I smiled at how happy Dylan looked with his boo. Even if the man was older than him by almost twenty years, he made Dylan happy. At the end of the day, that was all that mattered to me because he deserved it. As I looked at them, I couldn't help but wonder when I would find love. Don't get me wrong. There were a few men that wanted to be in my life. I didn't want to allow the wrong one to enter; he would only waste my time. Time was valuable and something you can never get back. So, I had no plans on wasting any of it.

A smile soon appeared as I thought about Ace. Although I had only seen him once at Myleena's place and a few times when he would escort her to and from class, I knew he was special. From the way that Myleena would say that he would defend her against LaToya told me that he was a good person. It told me that he didn't give a fuck about titles when it came to the two. He cared about right and wrong, which was very rare in this world, especially with Nitro technically being his boss.

My phone ringing brought me out of my thoughts as I looked down at it. I quickly answered once Myleena's name and picture flashed across the screen.

"Hey, gal," I greeted once the calls connected.

"Hey," she answered. "Are you busy?"

"Nah. I'm just getting home and eating some ice cream. What about you?"

"Nothing. Just finishing up another assignment from class. I was calling to tell you I couldn't make the study group tomorrow night."

"Oh really?" I asked. "Why not?"

"I forgot that's the night of Nitro's mother's party. I was invited to be Nitro's plus-one."

"Ohh, wee," I shouted as I damn near dropped my ice cream on my bed. "And how does Miss Bitch feel about that?"

"Oh, she's angry," she laughed. "Believe me."

"Was Ace invited?"

"I think so," she answered.

"Does he have a date?" I found myself asking before I could stop myself.

"I'm not sure. Why?"

"No reason," I replied with nervousness in my voice.

"You really like him, huh?" she asked.

"I hardly know him, but he is cute."

"Well, I'll be sure to keep an eye on him for you," she giggled.

"Don't make it sound like I'm sprung on him. I just think he's cute."

"I hear you," she said as she continued to laugh. "We can reschedule the study group for the next day. That is, if you're free. That way, I can tell you all about the party."

"I don't know. Let me talk to Dylan about it."

"I already did," she answered. "He said he's okay with the change."

"All right, then, booskie. I'll see you later. And I want to know *all* the details," I reminded her.

"You got it," she said with a laugh before disconnecting the call.

Once again, I found myself smiling at the thought of Ace. Here I was, gone off a nigga and didn't even know if he had a woman, or man, for that matter. If he didn't, that was a good thing for me, and if he did, I'd just keep it moving like I always did.

"I hope he's single," I prayed as I lay on my bed and stared at the ceiling. "I'm ready to find the one."

Chapter Fifteen

Nitro

I fixed my tie as I stared at myself in the mirror. Tonight was the night of my mother's fiftieth birthday party, and I was more than ready to celebrate it with her. With her beating breast cancer twice and other illnesses, her reaching her fiftieth birthday was nothing short of a blessing, and we all knew it. I also knew the time and effort that my father had put into making this night for her special made it all the more of a reason for everything to go as planned.

I admired my new custom-made suit, and although I usually wore black on black, the wine red actually pulled my entire look together. With a fresh taper and a fresh line-up, I was looking damn good, if I did say so myself. Through the mirror's reflection, I saw my phone continuously lit up. Walking over to my shit, I immediately saw LaToya's name and picture flash across the top of the screen.

Not in the mood for her antics, I sent her to voicemail. I already knew she was still upset about not being invited to the party, but as I had previously told her, this was a night for my mother. Unfortunately, my mother didn't care for her. So, the last thing that I wanted to do was upset my mom and ruin the night. If that meant I had to disappoint or make LaToya unhappy to keep a smile on my mom's face, then that's just what it had to be.

I walked over to my dresser and sprayed my favorite Perry Ellis cologne before placing my phone in my pocket and leaving my bedroom. I sat in the living room, checked last night's game scores, and waited for Myleena to appear. I'd be lying if I said I wasn't anxious to see her tonight. Donny had been in her room for two hours getting her ready. When he dropped off my suit, I managed to get a small glimpse of her dress, and from what I could see, it was definitely a lot different than what I was used to her wear.

It seemed as though just as those thoughts crossed my mind, Donny was making his way down the steps.

"Well, don't you look nice," he said as he entered the living room. "I did a damn good job on the colors. Y'all are going to look so good together."

"What are you talking about, Donny?" I asked with raised eyebrows.

"Don't worry. You'll see," he replied with a wink. "Just call me your fairy godmother because I definitely turned Ms. Myleena into your Cinderella for the evening. She's just putting on the last touches, but believe me, you're going to be one envied man when they see the gem on your arm tonight," he said before walking out the door.

If I were anxious before, I was more than anxious now. I kept looking at the time on my watch as I continuously glanced at the stairs. Although we were on schedule, it felt like she took forever to come down the steps. My phone vibrating in my pocket briefly distracted me. Pulling it out of my pocket, I answered it without even checking who was calling, already knowing it was no one but LaToya.

"What the hell do you want?" I spat. "You already know what tonight is, and I'm not in the mood for none of your shit."

"Chill out, dog. It's Ace."

Looking down at the screen, I shook my head. Having to deal with LaToya's ass was really knocking me off my square.

"My bad, Ace. Wassup?"

"Nothing. Just checking on yo' status."

"I'm just waiting on Myleena right now. After she's ready, we'll be on our way."

"Well, I'm already here. Guests are arriving. Yo' mom and pops are en route. So, y'all better get here before they do," he said before hanging up.

Knowing how my parents were about time, I knew we couldn't get there after they made their grand entrance. Besides, it was their party.

"Myleena!" I called out. "We gotta get going."

I heard the sounds of her heels clicking across the floor upstairs. Looking up as she walked down, my eyes bulged, and my mouth dropped to the floor. She looked nothing short of stunning as she wore a long-sleeved, wine-red dress with a slit up her thigh that showcased her well sculpted legs. She matched me perfectly. Not to mention that the dress was nicely complimented with a pair of diamond-encrusted stilettos that showed off her freshly French manicured toes.

I practically drooled at the sight of the dress as it clung to her body and looked like it was painted on her. I silently admired her slim frame as the dress showed off her ample breasts, slender waist, and thick hips. The body that she usually kept hidden was now on full display. Her hair, which she usually kept covered, now hung in loose curls past her shoulders and stopped at the middle of her back.

I had to be sure to up Donny's commission for the job he had done on her. He was right. She was going to be the most beautiful woman at the party tonight.

"What do you think?" she asked slowly. "I told Donny I think it might be a bit much."

"You look perfect," I replied, causing a smile to appear on her face.

I grabbed her by the hand and held it close as we walked out of my house and to my car. I could tell she was nervous by how she kept her eyes on the ground. Spinning her on her heels, I lifted her head and forced her to look me in the eyes.

"No more holding your head down," I spoke. "You're beautiful, and you're strong. Always have your head up."

"Thank you," she replied.

"No need to thank me. It's the truth. I don't want you to think about anything tonight. Not school, not homework, and not anything that happened in the past. You're out with me tonight, and we'll enjoy it."

Under the light, I could see the tears as they threatened to fall. I quickly grabbed the handkerchief from my pocket and dabbed them away.

"No crying. You look beautiful," I repeated once a smile finally replaced the tears. "Now, let's go and have some fun."

Chapter Sixteen

LaToya

I stared at the computer as yet another CNA health video played on the screen before me. I glanced down at the corner of the screen where the time was displayed. I was sure that this would be around when Nitro would be getting ready or even when he would be leaving for the party. Him and that little broken-English bitch Myleena. It didn't help that he wasn't answering my phone calls either. In fact, it only made the wheels in my head turn even faster.

As I stared at the computer screen, I could hear the words that the paid actors were saying, but I just couldn't focus for some reason. All I could think about was what they were doing. What was she wearing? Did she look good in her dress? Was she purposely showing off for my man? The Myleena I met a few months ago wasn't the same Myleena that she was today. The Myleena that used to be afraid to show her wrists now shows her arms and legs.

She was slowly but surely coming out of her shell and losing what little bit of her family religion that she had left. She was losing more of her Pakistani ways and becoming more American. Nitro and Ace saw it as a good thing, but I saw it as a threat. A threat to me and a threat to my place as Nitro's woman. Any bitch who I saw as a threat was a threat that had to be eliminated by any means necessary.

She really thought that I didn't know that she was trying to make a move on my man, but when it came to Nitro and my place in his life, I was far from being a dumb bitch. My eyes darted over to the door that led to the nurse's station just as the doors swung open. I rolled my eyes as Naomi pranced her lily-white ass inside.

"Hey, LaToya. Mrs. Jackson just had a blowout," she announced with a smile. "I rolled her into her room because she was starting to smell up the hallway."

"I'll take it as either you're blind and don't see what I'm doing, or you're just being a lazy bitch," I spat, not once taking my eyes from the screen.

"I think the one of me being a lazy bitch would be the most accurate choice," she spat back while mean mugging me. "Besides, she's technically *your* resident tonight."

I rolled my eyes to the ceiling, pushed myself away from the computer desk where I had once been sitting, and stood up. As I walked toward the door, I saw from the corner of my eyes Naomi glaring at me with a smirk plastered across her face. I knew that this was only get back from the other night, but I would die before I gave her the satisfaction of knowing that she was getting up under my skin.

I was sure to bump into her on my way out the door. Just as soon as I walked out of the nurse's station, the smell of shit hit me right in the face. Just the smell of it made me want to say fuck Mrs. Jackson and fuck this job, but knowing that I didn't want Nitro to know that I needed him kept me from putting in my two weeks' notice months ago. Like my mother once told me, you never show a man your true colors until after the ink is dry on your marriage certificate.

I tried my best to ignore the smell as I walked to Mrs. Jackson's room, but the closer I got, the stronger the smell became. Just as I made it to her door, my phone rang. Thinking that it was Nitro returning my call, instead of going into Mrs. Jackson's room, I dashed to the door that led to the courtyard.

"Hello, Nitro," I sang into the phone.

"Naw. Not Nitro. It's Bruno."

I immediately recognized the voice of my younger cousin, and instead of that happy feeling I once had at the thought of hearing Nitro's voice, I now felt irritation and frustration.

"What the hell do you want?" I spat harshly. "You know we only speak in person. Why are you calling me?"

"I'm calling to tell you that everything is in place. By the end of the night, you'll be the first in line for the queen of the throne, and I'll be one rich motherfucker," he squealed.

"Keep your fucking voice down. If one word of this shit gets out and to the wrong person, that's gonna be both of our asses. I don't know about you, but I ain't trying to die because of your fuckups."

"Believe me, big cuz, there's too much money on the line. I ain't fucking this up. So, consider it a done deal."

"Good. Don't call me again. Meet me at the spot at midnight tomorrow," I said before quickly disconnecting the call.

I smiled as I walked back into the building. The feeling and thought of this CNA life being behind me and the life of being the girl and possibly the wife of a kingpin sent me on a high so good that I no longer could smell the shit on Mrs. Jackson.

I walked out of her room after making sure that she was good. As I went down the hall, I looked toward the dining area. As expected, Naomi was doing her usual late-night lunch date with Joe.

I was no longer feeling petty enough to fuck up her night. In fact, I felt so good that my dream of being the queen of New York was about to become a reality that I did my rounds early and with a big smile. The way I saw it was, why not smile? Soon, all of this was going to be funny. I sat back at the nurse's station after completing my rounds and scrolled through my Instagram as I sipped on my bottle of water.

The hours ticked away like minutes, and I was still scrolling and liking pictures, but after a few scrolls, I damn near spit out the water that filled my mouth as a picture of Myleena caught my eye. It was none other than a picture of her with Nitro at his mother's birthday party, but it wasn't the fact of her being at the party with Nitro that shocked me because I already knew that much. It was what she was wearing. She looked better than any fucking model that I had ever seen. If I were completely honest with myself, she looked better than me. The way that dress was hugging her body was amazing. In fact, she didn't look like the same girl.

Looking at the top of the picture, I could have shitted a fucking brick at who posted the photo.

"Damn it, Bruno," I yelled as I banged on the table in front of me. "I knew you would find a way to fuck this shit up," I fussed.

For a nigga who wasn't even supposed to have been there, he was actually making himself seen enough to post a fucking picture and have it on his newsfeed. At that moment, I regretted everything. I regretted making the plan, I regretted setting it up, and I damn sure regretted getting Bruno to be the one to do it. My hands shook uncontrollably as I repeatedly dialed his number to call it off, but I was sent straight to voicemail every time I called.

After about a hundred times, I gave up. I took deep breaths as I tried to calm myself down. This nigga had just committed the dumbest crime of a lifetime. Rule number one in doing crime was if you're gonna do it, you had to do it right.

"Damn. What am I gonna do now?" I asked as all thoughts of being queen went out the window.

If word got out that Bruno was behind this hit and I was the puppet master, my days on this earth would be numbered. I ran to the bathroom as a wave of nausea came over me, but I knew I wasn't sick. I felt nauseated at the fact that I had basically just signed my own death certificate. It was one thing to fuck with the devil, but it was another thing to get caught.

Chapter Seventeen

Myleena

I clung to Nitro's arm as he led the way through the grand ballroom. It was beautifully decorated in shades of burgundy and gold and was filled with people. I'd always dreamed of going to parties like this. These were the kind of parties that my mom often told me about without my father knowing. According to her, those were some of the best times of her life.

"Would you like something to drink?" Nitro asked as he turned to face me.

"Please."

He smiled at me as he once again led me around the room. It seemed as though people flocked to him as we glided across the floor. I quietly stood beside him as he made small talk with a few of them. Once again, I felt small as I stood in this room filled with people, but the occasional smile that Nitro would give me told me that he was right there with me. Something about his smile made me feel safe by his side.

We saw Ace just as we made it to the bar. He wore a smoky-gray suit with black accents. His dreads were pulled into a messy but good-looking bun at the top of his head. He approached us as soon as our eyes landed on each other, but I couldn't ignore the woman who followed closely behind him as he walked over to us. My grip on Nitro's arm got tighter as my eyes connected with the gun that was perched on Ace's waist.

"It's okay," Nitro said as if he could read my mind.

"I thought y'all would never get here," he said to Nitro while staring at me. "You look beautiful, Myleena."

"Thank you," I blushed. "You don't look too bad yourself."

"What can I say?" he asked cockily. "I clean up nice when I have to."

"And who is your date?" I asked as I looked behind him at the woman standing off to the side.

"I never bring a date," he smiled. "That's just Unique. She's Donny's assistant. We were actually just looking for him. I have a few people who are interested in working with him."

"Well, I'm sure he'll be happy to hear that," I replied.

Even though I was talking to Ace, I just couldn't let go of Nitro's arm for some reason. As Ace began to speak to Nitro, out of the corner of my eye, I noticed a small crowd forming at the room entrance.

"Looks like Mom and Pops arrived," Nitro whispered in my ear. "Let's go over and say hello."

I smiled at him and nodded as we walked over to where the small crowd had formed. The people made room for Nitro and me as we made our way to the front. We instantly saw his parents, who looked like Michelle and Barack Obama, waving to their guests. His mother was so beautiful as she stood before us, wearing an all-black dress. The dress fit her like a glove as it clung to her body, a body that most women would pay millions of dollars to have. As soon as they greeted their guests and their eyes landed on Nitro and me, they made their way over.

"Well, don't you two look lovely," his mother said with a smile. "Almost as if you two belong together."

"Ma, don't start," Nitro replied as he looked at me.

"I'm serious, Nitro. She complements you very well. Way more than what's-her-face."

"Valentina," Nitro's father said. "Don't start."

"I'm only stating a fact," she replied.

I couldn't help the smile and laugh that escaped my lips from her comment. Whenever I met Mrs. Johnson, she never failed to mention or express her disdain for LaToya.

"LaToya, Ma," Nitro said as he squeezed my hand. "Her name is LaToya."

"Yeah, I remember."

"How about we change the subject?" Nitro's father interjected. "Tonight is all about you. Enjoy your night, my love."

Moments later, the DJ switched the music to a slow song, and Nitro's parents took it to the dance floor. Everyone was in awe as they glided across the floor in each other's arms, and we soon followed. My body melted as Nitro wrapped me in his arms. Slowly, we swayed to the soft beat of the music. I was in a complete daze as I wrapped my arms around his neck and stared into his eyes.

"Are you enjoying yourself?" he asked.

"I am. Thank you."

"For what?"

"For bringing me. For being such a good person to me . . . for everything."

We stared at each other and swayed in harmony for what felt like forever, but as our swaying continued, our faces drew closer and closer. It was as if our hearts were talking to each other. I smelled the champagne mixed with mint on his breath, sending my body into a whirl-wind. Before I knew it and before I could stop it, our lips touched. I knew it was wrong for me to kiss him when he was with LaToya, but it felt so right in my heart, and I'd be lying if I said that I didn't want it to end. His hands caressed my body as his tongue gently forced its way into my mouth. Although I had no idea what I was doing, I went with it. I sucked gently on his tongue as he swirled it around before my tongue began to do the same. It felt like absolute magic.

The song soon ended, and we heard clapping. Looking around, I now saw that all eyes were on us as we stood in the middle of the dance floor with his parents on the sideline.

"Oh my gosh!" I said as I stepped away from him. "I'm so sorry," I said before rushing off.

I couldn't get out of the room fast enough, so I bumped into people and tried to get away from him. Tears filled my eyes as I rushed through the bathroom door and into a stall. I silently cried as I thought about what I had done. My father would have had my head if he were alive to see what I had just done.

Knocking on the stall door made me pull myself together as I wiped away my tears. I came out of the stall, and Nitro's father met me as he held out a handkerchief.

"Thank you," I said as I slowly took the cloth from his hands.

"No problem," he replied, stepping back and allowing me to walk out.

I then walked over to the sink and looked at my face. Thankfully, I didn't smear my makeup too badly. I lightly dabbed at the running mascara around my eyes until I was presentable before I saw Mr. Johnson still standing there. But upon closer examination, I realized that he wasn't looking as if he were concerned with worry. He appeared to have questions for me.

"Is there something wrong?" I asked. "I know that Nitro is with LaToya. I don't know what came over me just now. I'm so sorry," I cried.

"That's not what I'm concerned about," he said as he placed his hand in the air to silence me. "I've meant to speak with you for a while now."

"About what?"

"You see, it's been months since the death of your father, my best friend, and although I have the tapes, I still can't seem to see how it all happened. I've known your father for many years, and he's always been a careful man. He has always carefully calculated and evaluated every move that he's ever made, which has led me to believe that his murder was an inside job . . . maybe even personal."

It was then that the dots began forming. Now I realized that he was accusing me of murdering my parents and younger sisters.

"So, you really think that I am capable of killing my father?" I yelled as I threw the handkerchief that he offered to the ground.

Rage filled my eyes as the tiny piece of fabric landed at his feet. My father always told me that other than spitting on someone, throwing something at a man's feet was the ultimate sign of disrespect, but at this point, I couldn't have cared less. In fact, I wanted to disrespect him just as much as he was disrespecting me at this moment.

"Did you?" he asked casually.

"For what reason would I have?"

"Like I said, I knew Don very well. I knew that he was strict with you and your sisters. Maybe you killed him because you wanted more freedom."

In the beginning, I was crying from embarrassment, but now, I cried tears of anger. The more I looked at him, the more I regretted the entire night. Now, I wished more than anything that I would have stayed in the room with my family instead of going to my room. Then I would be with them and happy rather than miserable here.

"Yes, my father was strict. And yes, I wanted more freedom, but never would I have killed him for it!" I screamed as more tears poured down my face. "I loved my family more than anything. More than money, more than happiness, and more than freedom, and I'd do anything to bring them back or avenge the person who took them away from me."

Then I finally spoke about the thoughts I had held ever since that night that everything happened. I never broke eye contact with him as I shared my deepest and darkest feelings. Moments later, his eyes softened, and he wrapped his arms around me as I cried into his chest. With my father's last words telling me not to cry and to be strong, it was at this time that I realized I was never given the time to mourn. To mourn the death of my mother, the death of my father, the death of my sisters . . . and the death of the only life that I had ever known.

"It's all right, Myleena," he whispered, stroking my hair.

"No! It's not all right!" I yelled as I snatched away from him. "You just accused me of murdering my family!"

"I just had to be sure," he replied softly. "I'm sorry."

I did nothing but stare at him for what seemed like an eternity. I wanted to forgive him, and although I knew and understood that his only motive was to find who was responsible for my family's murders, it didn't make it any less painful. I glanced down as he held his hand out for me to take. Together, we walked out of the bathroom where Nitro was waiting.

"Is everything okay?" he asked as he looked from me to his father.

"Yes," I replied with a smile.

"Everything is good, son," Mr. Johnson reassured him before walking away.

Nitro walked over to me and once again wrapped me in his arms. I still couldn't bear to look at him. Some would say that I was still embarrassed, but if I were to be honest with myself, I would say it was because I could no longer deny my feelings for him. Regardless of whether I liked it, I committed the deadliest sin in my father's eyes. I was falling in love with him.

"I'm sorry, Nitro."

"Don't be sorry," he replied, forcing me to look at him. "I wanted to do it too."

"You did?"

"I didn't pull back," he laughed.

Before we could speak any more, we heard his father calling everyone to gather around. Nitro pulled me by the hand as we approached where his father stood. With champagne flutes in hand, he made a toast.

"This is to my beautiful wife, who, with each year, makes me realize how and why I fell in love with her."

I smiled as I looked at them. How they looked at each other with so much love and adoration in their eyes was such a beautiful thing. Their love reminded me so much of the love that my parents once shared. I wished I would find the same kind of love someday. I looked around the room at the crowd as they continued to look at Mr. and Mrs. Johnson.

As I stared into the crowd, I couldn't take my eyes off two men as they made their way to the front of the room. I noticed them because, unlike the rest of the crowd, they weren't smiling. Unlike everyone else, they weren't happy about the joyous occasion that this was. Then I looked down and saw the guns they carried. My heart dropped to the floor as I followed where they were heading with my eyes.

As Mr. Johnson continued to profess his love for his wife, all I could see were my parents. All I could think about was how much I missed them and wished I had done something that night. It was as if life was moving in slow motion as I raced to the front. It was as if time had frozen as they aimed their guns, and others who saw the weapon ran for shelter. In my heart, it was as if this were my chance to do it all over again. God was giving me another opportunity to save my parents . . . one last chance to save my family.

Shots rang out.

I instantly felt a burning sensation as I fell to the floor. My entire body felt as if it were on fire. I looked up at the ceiling as people rushed around me. Bullets ripped the air, I felt someone lift my body from the ground.

"Myleena!"

I heard my name being called as my body began to shake uncontrollably. Looking over, I smiled as I saw my father's face again.

"Don't worry, Myleena. Help is coming. You just stay here with me," he repeated.

"It's okay, Daddy," I said as I began to cry, and blood filled my mouth. "I saved you" was all I could think to myself. "I saved you this time," I struggled to say as I choked on my blood.

Thoughts of happiness and being able to save my father were my last thoughts before my body ran cold and my world went black.

Chapter Eighteen

Willie Moe Johnson

"I want a twenty-four-hour watch outside of these gates at all times!" I yelled at every man who was under me. "There should have been no way that they could've gotten this fucking close to me, let alone this close to my fucking wife!"

"Yes, sir," they all said as they nodded.

"There's no reason that the daughter of my best friend should be in surgery getting three bullets pulled out of her fucking chest!"

I couldn't describe the level of anger that I felt as I looked around the packed room. It was like something that I had never felt before. It was one thing to lose my best friend, but it was another thing to almost lose his daughter, who he made my responsibility to keep safe. I looked from them to my wife as she stood in the doorway. What was supposed to have been a night celebrating the life of my wife and also the night that I officially stepped from the throne as king turned into a night of bloodshed and a night that almost ended with Myleena's life being taken.

The look on Valentina's face as she followed me out of the conference room told me that she wasn't happy with my decision.

"Willie, now, you know I don't like them being here," she said as she followed me into the kitchen. "This is my house."

"I understand that, my love, but right now, it's a matter of life and death."

"I get that," she yelled. "You fail to remember that I'm not the good little housewife you like to paint me out to be. I wasn't always this Betty Crocker bitch in the kitchen making cookies from scratch. Don't you ever forget that I was once that bitch out there in the trenches with you, helping you get to where you are right now."

"I know that too, Valentina, and I'll never forget it, but if I have to choose between letting you be independent and protecting your life . . . You know which one it'll be, right?" I asked as I looked her dead in the eyes.

"And how do you know you can trust them?" she spat. "Where were they when them niggas tried to shoot at us? How were they even able to get into the building?" she asked.

"I don't know, but you better believe me when I tell you I'm gonna find out. When I do, I'm gonna end them and everyone attached to their bloodline."

"There's a leak in your ship, Willie, and it's up to you to find it and plug it," she said as she caressed my cheeks. "This is our shit. We built this. And I'll be damned if someone tries to take it from us." I understood what she was saying and could see the maliciousness behind her words. She made herself very clear. "I can protect myself, Willie. You have to trust me on that."

"Allow me to protect you, V," I said, calling her by her nickname. "We ain't in the same place where we were all those years ago. We don't have to get our hands dirty anymore. I got people for that. Just like I got people who are willing to lay down their lives and die to protect you, just like I would. Let me protect you, V," I said as I once again called her by her old street name.

It was the same nickname I used to call her when she ran the streets with me. As she said, she was right by my side while I made my serves and rose up the ranks. She was there with me every step of the way. She even laid a couple of niggas out who tried to take me out. She was a true rider. Valentina was a true queen, and I knew that after her, there would never be another for me who could fill her stilettos.

Her question continued to echo in my head. It was the same question that I had been asking myself ever since everything went down. How did they know when and where this party was? Looking at my beautiful wife, I couldn't imagine anything happening to her. I'd die before I allowed any harm to come to her. As she smiled at me, I thought back to the day that her smile hypnotized me and the day that I knew I had to make her mine . . . forever.

I took a deep breath as I looked over at my wife and kissed her softly. We'd been in the game for over thirty years, and it had been over thirty years that I ever had to do the things I was about to do now.

My duty as a husband and father was always to provide and protect my family. Throughout my time in the streets, I've been able to provide my family with the life of luxury that they have now. Now, as I walked down to my office and stared at my assortment of guns, I knew that it was time to protect them. I had to protect what we built. I had to protect what was ours.

I closed my eyes as I placed my gun on my waist and walked back up the stairs and out the door. Just as instructed, guards were lined up by every entry point of our home with guns in their hands. As I got in my car and drove to the hospital, my mind was clouded with visions of Myleena as she choked on her blood. My heart shattered at the fact that she took three bullets for my wife and me—even after I had accused her of murdering her own family. To say that I felt like shit would have been an understatement.

I gripped the steering wheel tightly as a vision of Myleena as she clung to life would forever be embedded in my mind. Her last words before she lost consciousness would forever haunt me.

I finally arrived at the hospital and rushed up to the fifth floor. I tried my best to remain calm as I stood in the elevator. Truth be told, I hated hospitals. I hated the smell of them. To me, they reeked of death. Finally, the elevator doors opened, and I immediately saw Nitro and Ace as they sat in the waiting room lobby. Once Ace saw me, he quickly stood up and approached me.

"How is she?" I asked.

"We're not sure. The nurse said that she's still in surgery."

"How's Nitro?" I asked as I looked over at my son, who was staring at the double doors in front of him.

"Not good. He blames himself for her being in here, but while he blames himself, I can only blame myself. I let my guard down."

"Don't," I replied sternly.

"It's my job to keep y'all safe. It's my job to stay on point. I fucked up."

"No. You were around family. Your guard should never have to be up when you're around family."

"But I have a job," he argued.

"And you still do," I replied. "We have a leak, and we need to find it and plug it up," I said before I walked over and sat next to Nitro.

He kept his eyes on the doors in front of him. Although I didn't know what was going on between him and

Myleena when I wasn't around or what had gone down to spark the kiss, I could see that he was distraught about her. Although he was a grown man, I still saw my son, who was hurting and needed comfort.

"Everything is gonna be okay, son," I said, more to myself than to him.

"I don't want to hear that," he replied while his leg shook. "I don't want to hear nothing from nobody but the doctor. I need to know that she's okay," he repeated.

Myleena's blood stained his suit, and thoughts of how he refused to let her go after she fell to the floor came to mind. I thought of how tightly she gripped my arm as she spoke to me before she lost consciousness.

The ringing of his phone caused us both to look down. A look that could only be described as pure irritation soon followed. He took a deep breath, pulled his phone from his pocket, and placed it to his ear.

"Wassup?"

He stood up as he walked away. It wasn't before long I heard him raising his voice at whoever he was talking to. That caused me to get up and walk over to him.

"LaToya, I ain't got time for yo' shit right now. Some shit went down tonight, and I ain't in the mood, and I damn sure don't have the time for yo' attitude," he said before he disconnected the call and placed the phone back in his pocket.

The sounds of the double doors opened, and two doctors emerged. My heart raced as they walked to the center of the room.

"The family of Ashik," they said as they looked around.

I stepped forward with Nitro right behind me. The doctors approached us. I took a deep breath before they began to speak.

"How is she?" Nitro asked quickly. "Is she gonna be okay?"

"Ms. Ashik is a lucky woman. The three bullets went in and out. Fortunately, none of them hit any of her vital organs."

"Thank God," I replied as a big weight of worry fell off my shoulders.

"Although she will be fine, she will be in a lot of pain for the next few weeks. So, I advise her to have limited movement and nothing too strenuous. I've prescribed her some pain medication to help alleviate the pain."

"Can we see her?" Nitro asked.

"She should be ready for visitors, but like I said, she's in a lot of pain. So try not to get her worked up. She's in room 506," the doctor said as they walked away.

I turned to look at Nitro, but he was already headed for the rooms. Ace and I followed behind him until we came to her door. Just the smell of the hospital made me want to throw up. The stale gray paint made it look more like a prison than a place of healing. We stood silently outside her room. Nitro was already walking through the doors, but I needed an extra minute for some reason. I couldn't bear to open the doors and see Myleena hooked up to any machines.

Ever since my own father died from multiple gunshot wounds to the chest, and his death was slow and painful, I've hated hospitals. I hated how the doctors only made him comfortable with doses of morphine until he finally slipped away. I hated how the balloons and flowers were only decorations for his grave before he was actually dead. I hated how my father was only a street mechanic and still died the way he did.

Unlike me, my father wasn't in the streets and never got his hands dirty in the sense of criminal activity. All he ever did was work on cars and try his best to help others in his community. Eventually, he was known for being a rich man. Unfortunately, people mistook what others meant when they called him "rich." And because of their ignorance regarding the kind of man that my father was, he was killed. But throughout our small neighborhood, my father was always a giver. A person who would give before he would take. In that sense, people called my father rich.

He was rich in honor and rich in love and respect. But someone from another hood mistook him for being rich in money. One night, after closing up the shop, he was held up at gunpoint and demanded to give some masked hoods money. When he told them that he didn't have any, they shot him eight times in the chest and left him for dead. It took my father two weeks of pain in the hospital before his body finally gave out. Sometimes, I believe that the reason why I started my career in the streets was because of my father's death. If I was gonna die by some bullets in the streets, I at least wanted to own them. Some would call me crazy, but in a way, it was my way to get closure.

I shook my head as I pulled myself from the painful memory that I spent my entire life trying to keep buried. I was never the type of person who liked to feel helpless and vulnerable. It wasn't until I fell in love with Valentina and had Nitro that I realized that sometimes, it's okay. Sometimes, it's just a part of being human.

I walked through the door, which was a task that was easier said than done. Upon opening the door, I was relieved. I was expecting to see Myleena hooked up to multiple machines, so I was surprised to see that she was only hooked up to two.

The few steps it took to reach her bed seemed much longer than they were. I looked down at her as she lay in the hospital bed, looking up at me. A smile spread across her face once our eyes locked, causing Nitro to look over at me. After thinking about the past few hours, I again felt the need to apologize to her for my previous accusations. I hated to feel vulnerable. But at the end of the day, I was a man. A man should never be afraid to say he's sorry for his actions.

"Myleena, I'm so sorry."

I held my head down in shame, something that rarely happened. I felt so bad that I could barely stand to look at her.

"It's okay," she replied softly as she reached for my hand. "It's okay," she repeated. "I'm okay."

"No, you're not," I argued.

"But I will be," she said with a smile, gripping my hand tighter. She looked so much like her father that it pained my heart to see her like this.

I tried my best not to shed a tear as I looked around the dimly lit room. When I looked down at her, all I could see now was Don. She was the spitting image of my best friend. All I could think about was how I wished that I had been there that night to save him and the rest of his family.

"Nitro, can you give us a minute?"

"Sure," he replied, walking away with Ace behind him.

I waited until I heard the door closing before I returned my attention to Myleena. There was so much that I wanted to tell her. So much that I felt like she needed to know. I took a deep breath and sat beside her bed in the chair.

"Your dad and I were friends for a long time," I began. "We often referred to each other as brothers. We started out in the streets together and rose up from there. We both knew the risks we were taking by doing what we could to provide for our families. Me providing for my wife, and him providing for your mother."

A tear rolled from my eye. I felt the warmth of the tear as it hit my cheek and slowly rolled down my face. I closed my eyes tightly as I tried to gather my thoughts.

"We always promised each other that if either of us were to get hurt or die, the other would carry on and look after our family. That was my promise to your dad, and with what happened to you tonight, I failed him," I said before completely breaking down. "Don't get me wrong, I've failed at plenty of things before, but this . . . This was the one thing I wasn't supposed to fail at."

"You didn't fail my father . . . You didn't fail me either. I'm still here. I'm here because of you."

Looking at her, I also saw the tears as they sat in the corner of her eyes. Her grip on me got tighter as her tears fell, but along with the question of who were the ones that pulled the trigger, there was another question that I desperately needed an answer to.

"Earlier tonight," I said, "before you lost consciousness . . . You called me dad. Why?"

"I saw him," she whispered. "I saw him in your eyes. There are so many things that I wish I would've done differently that night. So many things that I wish I could change. Saving you and your wife was more like me getting a second chance to save my mother, another chance to save my father."

Chapter Nineteen

LaToya

I looked around the living area as Naomi sat with Joe. While this bitch was having the time of her life with this Uncle Tom-ass nigga, I was damn near walking a hole through the floor as I paced back and forth across the area that served as the nurse's station. My nerves were shot to shit as I continuously dialed Nitro's line. After about the hundredth time of calling and being sent to voicemail, I couldn't take it anymore. I was really about to lose my shit, and I didn't mean figuratively.

Not only was my cousin now not answering his phone, but Nitro also wasn't either, which I didn't take as a sign from God. I took deep breaths to try to keep myself from hyperventilating. As I said, I knew the risks that I was taking by following through with this plan, but with me being blinded by jealousy and fear, I allowed myself to become one of the bitches that I only read about in books.

Going behind my man's back, I set up his mom and the woman he's supposed to be protecting to be killed. From the books that I've read, I now only saw this as going one way, but thinking that I was smarter than the bitches I read about, I was determined not to make the same mistakes that they did. Out of desperation, little did I know then I had just made the dumbest decision of them all. I hired a well-known, trigger-happy nigga that I knew couldn't hold water to hold one of my biggest secrets. A secret so big and dark that it could have my ass dead and my body never to be found. Not to mention the possibility of my entire bloodline being wiped from existence.

I closed my eyes as I tried to think of something—anything—that would get me out of this hellhole that I had dug for myself. Each time I closed my eyes, I imagined myself being tied up in a basement, screaming and being tortured for the part that I played in everything. I may not have been the one to pull the trigger, but I was damn sure the one who was pulling the strings. With me being with Nitro for as long as I had, I knew that being the bitch loading the clip was just as bad as the nigga who pulled the trigger and would receive the same death sentence as those involved. I screamed on the inside as my eyes shot open from the thought of seeing my body lying in a wet basement—lifeless. All because I hated to feel threatened. I couldn't do this shit. I just couldn't wait for death to come knocking on my door. I had to think of a plan to save my ass.

Grabbing my phone, I immediately called my supervisor. I had to get out of here. I had to see what was going on beyond these four walls. It felt like an eternity went by before my supervisor finally answered.

"LaToya," she said once the calls were connected.

"Yes," I replied, trying to keep my voice at an even tone. "How are you?"

"Do you have any idea what time it is? Did one of the residents have to be rushed to the hospital or something? Did one of them die?"

"No," I answered as I began packing my belongings.

"Well, what could possibly be the reason for you calling me this late at night?" she asked with attitude.

"I apologize for that, Francine, but due to a family emergency, I won't be able to finish my shift."

"Is everything okay?"

"I'm honestly not sure. I just got a call from my mother saying that she's being rushed to the emergency room, and with me being her next of kin, I need to be there just in case they ask questions or some decisions have to be made regarding her health," I lied quickly.

One thing that I loved about myself was that I was quick on my feet. I could rattle off a lie within seconds and make the shit sound so smooth that it sounded like pure gospel. Not to mention, I could cry at the drop of a hat just to put the icing on the cake and make my lies sound more believable. Thanks to my mother, it was a trick I had picked up early on. After watching my mother deal with her many men, I learned more than a few tricks to ensure I always got my way.

"I understand," she replied. "Is someone there with you?"

"Yes, Naomi is here."

"Okay, ask her if she can hold it down until around five. I can call and ask Amy to come in early this morning to finish up."

"Thank you so much," I said as I rushed for the door.

"No problem. Just take care of your mom and call me if you need anything," she replied before hanging up the phone.

A wicked smile spread across my face as I practically pranced my ass out of the nurse's station and over to where Naomi and Joe were sitting.

"Hey, Naomi," I said as I stood before them.

"What?" she asked while rolling her eyes in my direction.

"A family emergency just came up, so I won't be able to finish up the rest of my shift. I called Francine, and she said it's cool for me to leave and for you to hold it down until Amy gets here at five," I relayed all in one breath.

"You can't be serious," she fussed as she pushed Joe away from her. "How the hell does Francine expect me to take care of forty patients by myself?"

"Well, considering how they're all asleep, and I've already changed them, I think she figured you could hold it down for three hours. Besides, I'm sure if things get too hectic, Joe wouldn't mind assisting you," I replied smartly as I turned around and walked away.

I ignored Naomi and her smart-ass remarks and made a beeline toward the door. I wasted no time clocking out and walking to my car. I couldn't even enjoy the midnight breeze as I walked through the dark parking lot. As I approached my car, out of the corner of my eye, I saw a black truck in the far corner of the parking lot. Whoever was in the truck turned off their lights as I approached.

My heart raced as I snatched my keys from my purse and scrambled to my car. My keys shook uncontrollably as I tried to place them in the door. I couldn't get my nerves under control as I opened the door, put the key in the ignition, and started my car. After pulling from the parking lot, I tried to chalk up the reason for the truck in the parking lot to me just being paranoid, but something in my heart told me I wasn't.

I raced to a spot where my cousin Bruno was known for being at. I pulled up to Max's, a local hole-in-the-wall kind of bar that sat on a damn near abandoned street in one of the worst neighborhoods of the Bronx. As I stared at the building, which looked like it would fall down should the wind blow on it too hard, I regretted the last time I was here. It was a night that Nitro and I had gotten into another argument over Myleena. He made the bitch feel welcome when he should have been telling her that her welcome had run out.

It was a night that I was tired of going over there and smelling one of her nasty-ass foreign dishes. It was a night that I was just tired of keeping my disdain for her ass to myself. One word led to another, and the next minute, I was here with Bruno, complaining and venting about the women in my man's life. What started as a joke to make me feel better soon turned into a mistake that could cost me my life.

"Wassup, LaToya? You looking for Bruno?" someone asked.

"Yeah."

"He's in the back of the bar. Looks like he had a pretty rough night. As a matter of fact, it's a good thing that you're here. The way he looks, he'll need a ride home."

Once again, that feeling of regret rested in the pit of my stomach. Against my better judgment, I continued with my walk inside the building. I scanned the partially filled bar as I searched for Bruno. I spotted him within seconds as he sat at a table at the very back of the bar. Even through the poorly lit club, I could see his high-yellow ass as clear as day.

I could only shake my head at him as he sat at the table with his head down. With a bottle of liquor in one hand and his phone in the other, my blood boiled when he looked up to check his phone before placing his head back down. That alone told me that he was purposely ignoring me. No longer worried, I was pissed as I marched my way over to him and took a seat.

"Wassup, cuzzo?" I said sarcastically.

My sudden presence startled him as he dropped his phone and jumped up from his seat. Grabbing his gun, he aimed it in my direction. It wasn't until he realized that it was me that he felt safe enough to lower his weapon.

"My bad," he said quietly as he sat back down. "My ass been on edge since everything happened. When can you get me my money?"

"I'm not sure. I'm working on it."

"I don't need you to 'work on it,' Toya. I need that shit now. With everything that has gone down tonight, shit is gonna be real hot for me right now. I need to get the fuck outta Dodge."

"I get that, Bruno, but I can't give you something I don't have right now. Give me a few days," I replied as I felt myself growing more and more irritated.

"I might not have a few days, LaToya!" he shouted. "My fucking life is on the line. I just tried to get at Willie Moe's wife."

"Keep your motherfucking voice down," I spat as I looked around. "I said that I'd work on it. If you ain't patient enough to wait, you can carry your ass on, and I'll wire it to you when I get it. In the meantime, why don't you tell me just what the fuck happened tonight?"

"Don't worry about the details. Just know you got what you wanted."

"Not if his mother is still alive," I replied in a hushed tone.

"His mother might not be dead, but the bigger problem has been handled. I pumped three slugs into that other bitch's ass. No way she gonna live through that shit."

Looking around, I noticed that a few people, including the bartender, were now looking our way. Realizing how stupid we were and how suspicious we were looking, I knew that I had to get out of there before anything else could be said.

"Fine. Get up so I can take you home."

"Nah," he replied. "I ain't ready to leave yet. I still got a bottle that's half full."

"You don't need that damn bottle, and you're already pissy drunk. We both know that you have a bad habit of talking when you've been drinking."

"I can handle myself. Now, leave before you make me get loud," he threatened through clenched teeth.

"Fine. Don't let me hear that you been down here running your mouth to your little drinking buddies," I spat.

"Then cover yo' ears, and you won't hear shit," he replied in a drunken slur.

It felt like I couldn't get in my car fast enough. Having to walk past drunken women who were being carried away by men and being hassled for money by crackheads made me happy that I had clung on to Nitro long enough for him to get me out of the ghetto that I used to call home. I started my car and burned rubber down the street as I headed home.

The need to speak to Nitro washed over me as I dialed his number again. I prayed to God that he answered. I just needed to hear his voice. His voice alone would tell me if everything was okay or not. God must have been sitting next to the main line because my prayer was answered when I heard Nitro's sweet baritone.

"Wassup, LaToya?" he answered.

"Hey, baby. I've been calling you," I replied. "Is everything okay? How was the party?"

"I don't have time to talk right now. Some shit happened at the party, and Myleena was shot."

His voice sounded grave, but truth be told, I couldn't have cared less.

With fake concern, I said, "I'm so sorry to hear that, baby. Do you want me to come over to help you plan the funeral?"

"Funeral?" he asked. "Funeral for what? She ain't dead."

Chapter Twenty

Unknown

(One Day Later)

"What the fuck do you mean you didn't hit your target?" I yelled as I threw the shot glass that was once filled with Hennessey to the ground.

The glass broke into a million pieces as it shattered upon impact. Even the glass shattering wasn't enough to distract me from my rage. I swear these niggas were taking my leniency for weakness, and it was about time that I made an example out of one of their asses. I gripped the handle of my gun tightly as it lay on the table. I wanted so desperately to shoot these niggas, but the thought of me being the one to have to clean it up halted my actions, at least momentarily.

"The girl jumped in the way," Doc replied.

"What the fuck do you mean the girl jumped in the way?" I yelled. "What girl?"

"The girl that you told us to try to keep eyes on," he answered.

"I didn't ask you to try to do a damn thing. I told you to *do* it," I spat with rage.

"It's kinda hard to do that," he argued back. "She always got that dreadhead nigga around."

"Well, that nigga gotta go home sometime, and he damn sure gotta sleep sometime."

"No doubt, but if you get too close to where she been staying at, rumor has it that you're shot on sight," he informed me. "And no disrespect to you or Beast, but I ain't trying to get shot over no bullshit that don't really concern me."

To say that I was taken aback by his statement would have been putting it lightly. I was even more than shocked that he was stupid enough to have the balls to say some shit like that to me. These niggas really didn't believe me when I said that these streets and everything in them were soon going to be mine. Fuck Beast because I damn sure now had plans on getting rid of his ass too. A hurt woman was one thing, but a scorned and now dick-less one was on a completely different level. With that being said, I wasn't going to earn their respect. I was going to demand it. On the day I reign as queen, they could either bow down or lie down—simple as that.

"Shot on sight," I repeated as I felt myself change from Jekyll to Mr. Hyde. "Is that right?"

Blood splattered on the walls and on the tip of my Red Bottom stilettos as his body hit the floor with a hard thud. His eyes glazed as he looked at the ceiling before slowly closing. I smiled as I looked at the rest of the crew that attended the party with him.

"Is *this* what y'all want?" I asked as I gestured to the dead body that now lay at my feet. "Honestly, I don't feel like cleaning up the mess, but I'll damn sure make an exception before I take any more failures."

"Yes, ma'am," they replied.

I was more than just a little pissed that these mother-fuckers had shot Myleena. Although that was in my plans too, it wasn't supposed to have happened until the rest of her newfound friends and family were dead. I wanted her to die at *my* hands. I was like a snake in a tank. I like to play with my food a little bit before I execute my attack. Call me sick and twisted, but I wanted her to squirm a bit before I put her out of her misery.

"Is she dead?" I asked through narrowed eyes.

"We're not sure right now. I've been keeping my ears in the streets, and they're quiet, but—" he began before I cut him off.

"But what?"

"Were we the only ones that you had on the job?"

"*Excuse* me?"

"When we were there about to do the hit, I noticed a few other niggas in the party with guns too."

"Are you sure they weren't there for protection?" I asked smartly.

"Yes, ma'am," he answered as he nodded.

"And how are you so sure?"

"Because their guns also pointed at the intended target," he informed me.

Although I was shocked by this new information, it only made me wonder, and the wheels in my head turned faster. Who was after them? Who wanted them dead? In some famous words, "the enemy of my enemy is my friend." I stepped back and sat at the table as I looked at the group of men.

I tried to make the pieces to this puzzle fall into place. After doing my research in the streets, much to my dissatisfaction, I found out that Willie and his family were well liked and well respected throughout the community. In fact, most people considered them to be the hood version of the Obamas. That alone was the reason that I had to get some out-of-town niggas looking to expand their territory to team up with Beast and me to take over these streets.

"A'ight, well, here's the new plan. Lay off this hit. Right now, I want you to find out who them niggas were that tried to do the hit."

"And what do you want us to do when we find 'em?" one man asked as he looked around at the rest of the crew. "Kill them?"

"No. I want you to bring them to me."

"Yes, ma'am."

"Good," I said as I turned around, walked back to my chair, and sat down. "Dismissed."

I continued to think about the mysterious crew that took a shot at Willie and his family as my crew left the room. Then I looked down at Doc as blood seeped from his body. It was a mess. I took a deep breath of irritation and frustration as I walked to the bathroom. I quickly glanced at my reflection to ensure no blood was on my clothes.

I thought about the way this nigga spoke to me as if he were the HNIC. As I said, I had to make an example out of this nigga before the rest of these niggas thought that I was just a cute face with no malice behind my actions.

"You should have been smarter."

I looked back at him and then at my shoes and felt anger build up in me again. Only one thing could satisfy me at this point other than killing him again. I pulled and tugged on his body as I searched through his pockets until I found what I was looking for.

"Piece of shit," I yelled as I kicked the corpse. "This will go toward my replacement pair. You'll pay me in hell," I spat.

Twenty minutes later, I was making a call for the crew to dispose of the body, and Beast crossed my mind as I sat back in my chair. Usually, he was in attendance when we held a meeting regarding the progress of our business in the streets, but since his coming out party, he had been with Bone a bit more than usual. Most bitches would have been angry and ready to tear up some shit. Luckily for Beast, I was a different kind of bitch. I was a bitch of a different and rare breed. I was a bitch with a plan. The key to my plan was patience.

"Patience, baby girl," I said to myself as I swirled around in my chair. "Soon, everyone will know to fear you. They'll either fear for their life . . . or lose it."

Chapter Twenty-one

Nitro

It had been almost a week since the night that Myleena got shot at the party and three days since she's been released from the hospital. So much had changed. Myleena had gone from constantly being in the kitchen making her own meals to me having to escort her around and help her as much as possible. I'd be lying if I said I hadn't enjoyed it.

The doctors told us not to allow her to do strenuous activities, and I had gone above and beyond to ensure that she didn't, from carrying her schoolbooks to and from her room to helping her clean her stitches when Mrs. Valdez wasn't available. Although Ace was still around, I wanted to personally ensure that she was well taken care of. I wanted her to be in as little pain as possible since she didn't like to take the medicine to help ease the pain. She wouldn't take it unless the pain were unbearable, which was usually only at night since she would sometimes toss and turn in her sleep. I didn't understand why she didn't take the pills, but knowing how she had good reasons for everything else, I figured that this would be no different.

"No, Nitro. You gotta flip the chicken if you want it to be cooked evenly," Myleena giggled as she sat at the kitchen table.

"As long as it's cooked, and it ain't raw, that's all that matters," I answered while still doing what she said.

"No. It won't taste as good if it's cooked too much on one side and not enough on the other. Trust me."

"Trust you?" I questioned.

"Yes," she answered. "I'd never do you wrong."

Her comment caused me to look at her sideways as I tried to figure out what she meant. With her being around and living in my home for the past months, she'd had a front-row seat to my many arguments with LaToya, and the arguments had only gotten worse the past few days that Myleena had returned home. LaToya damn sure disapproved of me doing so much for Myleena during her recovery, but a known fact about her was she wasn't okay with anything that didn't benefit her in some way.

As the thoughts of LaToya crossed my mind, it caused me to jump back to the night of the party. For the life of me, I couldn't figure out why she would assume that Myleena was dead after the shooting. I might have been a bit paranoid because of their dislike of each other. Still, I had to figure out her reasoning for saying that because, in my mind, it was so far-fetched, especially with her not knowing where Myleena was shot and how she'd been acting lately. It wasn't the usual LaToya. Instead of her usual asking about shopping and shit like that, she now wanted to know more about the party and if I had any idea who the shooters were.

There were only two reasons that she could want to know more about what happened and who shot Myleena. One of those reasons was whether she had something to do with it or knew someone who did. The other reason was just to have something to gossip about to her friends, but with her knowing that I didn't like my personal business out in the streets, my mind was leaning more toward my first thought. Until I had proof to back up any claim,

I would give her the benefit of the doubt. I knew better than to come to any situation with half a clip.

"You're burning the chicken," Myleena yelled, snapping me from my thoughts.

"Oh shit," I yelled as I quickly took the food off the stove and set it on the counter.

I looked back over to a laughing Myleena. She was happy and smiling even when I knew she was in pain, which made me laugh too. The night of the shooting did something to me. It told me I genuinely had developed feelings for Myleena since she came to live here. Those feelings were what sparked the kiss. Through those feelings, I learned that I never wanted to see her get hurt again.

"I told you that this kitchen was only for decoration," I said as I placed the burning pan in the sink. "Until you came here, these pans had never been used."

"That's a shame," she replied.

The pan sizzled as I placed it under the stream of cold water. I laughed at how she actually had my ass in the kitchen cooking one of her foreign dishes. I thought I did pretty damn good with our breakfast this morning. It didn't matter that I had only popped a few mini pancakes inside the microwave. She enjoyed it, and to me, that was all that mattered. Now, she had me in here damn near about to burn my whole house down.

"I'm not a man for the kitchen," I said as I went to turn off the stove.

"Yeah, but what about Mrs. Valdez?" she asked. "Doesn't she cook for you?"

"Not really. She's more about keeping the place clean. LaToya normally likes to eat out."

"Why are you with her?" Myleena asked before quickly trying to take it back. "Oh, I'm sorry. Please forgive me. I know that's none of my business."

"No. You're good," I replied as I went to sit beside her. "You can ask me anything."

As I said those words, I sat back and thought of the question myself. Why *was* I with her? She didn't do anything for me. She couldn't do anything for me that I couldn't do for myself, and she damn sure didn't make my life any easier. In truth, she made my home life more difficult than my life in the streets. As I thought more about that question, I thought of my parents. They had been together for such a long time. It only made me wonder if I would ever find the woman I wanted to be with for the rest of my life.

"Nitro," Myleena said again, dragging me from my thoughts.

"Yeah?" I answered.

"If you were trapped on an island, would you take LaToya or a book?" she asked.

A look of confusion washed over my face at her question. It was a question I'd never been asked before and, in a way, didn't make any sense to me.

"I don't know. Why?"

"It was a question that my father was asked by his father when he met my mother," Myleena replied.

"And what was his answer?"

"He chose my mother. He said that if they were both trapped on an island, he knew that my mother wouldn't just sit there and wait for him to figure out what to do. He said that he knew she would be right beside him with a spear in her hand ready to hunt with him. At that moment, he told me he knew he had found a partner and not just someone who was with him to gain. Someone willing to help him build."

Damn was all that I could say as I pondered over what she said. I knew that, in more ways than one, LaToya meant no good to me. Most days, I questioned why I was with her and had been with her for as long as I had. For some reason, I could never come up with an answer, but now, as I stared at Myleena, it became more apparent than ever.

"Can I ask you a question?" I asked.

"Sure."

I looked deeply into her eyes as I sat next to her. Those gray eyes that she possessed were something so beautiful. So mesmerizing. So captivating.

"The night of the party, when we kissed," I began, "why did you do it?"

"I told you that it was a mistake," she replied, looking away from me. "I shouldn't have done that."

"No, it wasn't," I said, reaching over the table and forcing her to look at me. "You just said that you won't do me wrong. So, that means you can't lie to me."

She stared back at me with a tear in her eyes before blinking it away. A few seconds went by before she finally began to speak.

"I feel myself being drawn to you. I know that it's wrong, and I know what my father would have done to me if he were here right now, but I can't help myself. I feel myself falling for you, even with LaToya being your woman. I see you're a good person and have a heart of gold. I hear many stories about you in class from Dionne and Dylan about what you do for a living, and I don't judge you. How could I? The way you make your fortune is how my dad made his, and I loved my dad with everything in me. I hear people say that you're a monster in the streets. But even if that's who you are in the streets, that's not what I see when I look at you . . . and that's what I love."

Damn, that word *love* spoke volumes. Call me stupid or naïve, but for some reason, when she said it, I believed her. I believed her when she said that she loved me. Deep in my heart, I knew that the feeling was mutual. Initially,

I looked at her as nothing other than a mission, but now, I look at her as more than that. LaToya and I had been together for years, and the word "love" had never escaped our lips, but here I was with Myleena, a woman I hadn't known for as long as I'd known LaToya, and she loved me. Even when she knew that it was wrong and against her religion, she was willing to take that risk to say those words.

"I feel myself falling in love with you," she continued.

"How do you know that?" I asked.

I'd never said these words to anyone but my mother and father in all my years of living. I had no reason or need to. Showing love in these streets was a death sentence. In these streets, people allowed the word "love" to pull on their heartstrings. Those same strings would be why people ended up on the wrong side of the dirt. I could never allow myself to take that risk . . . until now.

"I think about you all the time. I pray for you more than I pray for myself. I pray for your protection. I pray for your peace. I pray for your sanity. I pray for your well-being. I want what's best for you. I feel my heart break at the very thought of something happening to you."

"How do you feel right now?" I asked as I slid closer to her.

She looked away from me as my hand grazed her leg before she looked back at me.

"I'm feeling . . . I'm feeling . . ." she said as she looked around the kitchen. "I'm feeling hungry," she said before a smile broke on her face. "And you burned the last of the chicken."

Sensing that she wasn't ready to admit to herself what she was already telling me, I decided to leave it where it was until she was ready. I just hoped that it wouldn't take too long.

"Well then," I replied with a smile as I pushed myself away from the table, "allow me to grab a few takeout menus. What you got a taste for?"

"I have a taste for something different," she answered. "So, just surprise me."

Thirty minutes later, we were piled up in the living room with food stacked on the coffee table. Although I preferred that people not eat in the living room, I made an exception for her. Thankfully, her teachers were okay with her doing her work during the week and turning it in on Fridays, at least until she recovered. With her school-work keeping her busy and the television keeping me company, I occasionally turned to look at her. I would be lying if I said she didn't look attractive with her glasses on and her head deep in the books. She looked so focused as she flipped back and forth between the pages.

"So, what do you want to be when you get out of school?" I found myself wanting to know.

"At first, I wanted to be a lawyer, just in case my dad ever needed me," she said with a giggle. "But now, with everything going on in the world, I think I want to be a surgeon," she answered with a smile.

As she said those words, for some reason, it made me think of LaToya and how they were so different. Myleena was so driven, knew what she wanted, and wasn't afraid or lazy to put in the time to get it. Once upon a time, LaToya wanted to be a nurse, but after seeing how much hard work and time it took, she decided to take an easier job as a residential assistant. She didn't even have the gumption to take her state board test to make the shit official, even after I offered to pay for it. Although LaToya was a bitch, I still wanted her to succeed and prosper in life, but all she wanted to do was shop and waste her time.

"I'll be right back," she said as she placed the book she was reading between us.

She struggled to get up, but she powered through the pain and did it. My eyes couldn't help but wander down her curvy frame. Since the night of the party, she has become less shy about showing her body while she is around the house. The body that was usually covered was now being shown off. I was mesmerized at how the biker shorts that she was wearing squeezed her curves and showcased her ass and legs.

"Damn," I said as I shook my head in amazement, but that still didn't make me stop looking at her ass and hips as they swayed from side to side.

My phone ringing pulled me from the trance that her walk had me in. Picking up my phone as it sat on the coffee table, my eyebrows furrowed in confusion as my mother's name popped up on my screen. She rarely called me on my cellphone because she usually only ever called the house. Sometimes, I wondered if she even remembered that I had a cellphone.

"Hello," I said once the calls were connected.

"Nitro!" she screamed. "They shot him!" she cried. "They shot him!"

"Who, Ma?" I asked as I began to panic. "They shot who?"

My heart dropped as I heard my mother cry. My mother has always been known to be a very strong and proud woman. So, in all my years of living, I've never heard her cry . . . until now.

"Your father!" she cried. "They shot your father! He's at the hospital!"

The phone fell from my hands and hit the floor as her words registered in my head. My heart raced as I felt my blood begin to boil. I knew that my father was a man made of flesh, but at the same time, I never thought that he would ever get hurt or, in this case, shot. I had always considered my father invincible, but this news shattered those thoughts. I was beyond shocked at the news that someone was once again able to get this close to my father to do him harm because he was always aware of his surroundings and was sure never to have his back facing a door or window. So, the fact that someone was able to get the drop on him told me that whatever the motive was behind these shootings, it was personal, and whoever was behind it wanted blood—our blood.

I could still hear my mother screaming as I looked back down at my phone. For the first time in my life, I felt fear. I felt fear, knowing that, once again, someone had gotten close to my family. This time, they succeeded.

"Nitro."

Looking over, I stared at Myleena as she stared from me to my phone, which was still on the floor.

"Is something wrong?"

"My father," I replied. "He's been shot," I said, still in shock.

I looked at her. Her mouth was moving, but I couldn't hear or register anything she said.

"I gotta go," I said as I jumped up from the couch. "I gotta go and see about my father."

"Do you want me to go with you?" she asked with concern.

"No, you stay here. I'll get Ace to come and watch the house," I said as I grabbed my phone from the floor. "Take this!" I instructed as I reached inside the drawer in the hallway.

Her eyes grew wide as I handed her an all-black .22 Springfield handgun.

"I can't," she said as she shook her head.

"You can, and you will."

"I'll be safer if I go with you."

"No, you won't," I replied. "With me not knowing who's behind this, you'll be safer here. Ace has a key. If anyone else comes through that door, shoot first," I instructed as I ran out.

It was pouring rain as I raced to my car. My mind went a mile a minute as I weaved in and out of traffic. My heart pounded, and my thoughts were in such a whirlwind as I sped through the city, making the usual thirty-minute trip in twenty. I damn near hit a man who was also being escorted into the hospital by a gurney. My car was barely in park before I jumped out and ran inside the emergency room entrance.

I felt as helpless as a kid who lost his parents at a store as I bumped and pushed people out of my way and headed toward the registration desk.

"How can I help you, sir?" the lady asked.

"Willie Johnson," I replied. "What room is he in?"

Chapter Twenty-two

Valentina

I gripped my husband's hand as I sat at his bedside. I tried my best not to cry, knowing he'd tell me to lift my head. I smiled as I looked at him. We had been together for so many years.

"Come on, baby," I said as I kissed his hand. "You gotta pull through this. We've been together too long. We've been through too much for me to lose you now."

As I stared at him lying peacefully on the hospital bed, my mind went back to when I first met him, back before we were what we are today. I smiled as I remembered the first time that I laid eyes on Willie Moe Johnson. He was just a small-time hustler then, and so was I. Willie was hustling to take care of his mother and him. I was just trying to eat. Where Willie was trying to take care of his mother after the brutal murder of his father, I, on the other hand, was tired of going home to a house with no lights, a refrigerator with no food, and having to boil water on the stove just to have warm water to wash my ass with.

Willie taught me the game, not only how to play it but also how to survive it. Together, we hustled and survived and built the multimillion-dollar empire it is today. I would be lying if I said I could have done it without him. He was my right hand and owned half of my heart, so I couldn't lose him. Not right now, not like this, but with me being with Willie for as long as I had, I knew that now wasn't the time for tears. Now was the time for action.

I took slow, deep breaths and swiped at the tear that wanted to fall. As much as I wanted to sit here and cry for my husband, I couldn't. I had to keep going. It's what he would have wanted. I turned around toward the door when I heard some commotion. I jumped up at the sound of my son's voice. Knowing Nitro and how he could be when he didn't get answers, I rushed from the room and followed the sound of his voice.

I turned the corner leading to the emergency room's front entrance. Rushing over, I placed my body between Nitro and the security guard he was fighting off.

"What's going on here?" I asked as I looked from Nitro to the officer.

"Do you know this man?" the white cop asked with his hand now placed on the handle of his gun.

"Yes," I answered, sure to keep my eyes on his hands. "He's my son. His father has just been shot."

"Yes, ma'am. I understand that. I just wanted to be sure that he had the right to be here."

"He does," I replied with narrow eyes.

I kept my eyes on the officer as he turned around and walked away. Grabbing Nitro by his shirt, I led the way back to his father's room. We didn't have time for Nitro to get arrested for putting his hands on a cop, and I damn sure didn't need them breathing down our necks if that were to happen, either.

"What's going on?" Nitro asked as he stopped in the middle of the hallway. "What's going on with Pops?"

I took a deep breath as I prepared to tell him what had happened to his father. In all honesty, I blamed myself. If it weren't for me being so ignorant and wanting to be so independent, Willie would've paid more attention to what was happening. I put my head down in shame. If Willie didn't pull through, I would forever blame myself.

"He was shot eight times," I answered.

My heart once again shattered as I said those words. Like I said, if it weren't for me, we wouldn't have been out in the open for so long for them niggas to let off shots.

"He was shot four times in the chest, twice in the legs, once in the arm, and one bullet grazed his head."

"How?" was all that Nitro could say.

"Everything happened so fast," I replied, replaying everything in my head. "One minute, we were arguing, and the next minute, bullets were in the air. I fired back as they turned the corner, but when I looked for your father, he was already on the ground," I said as I allowed the tears that I had been holding back to fall freely.

"What are the doctors saying?"

"They were able to remove the bullets or at least most of them, but during the surgery, while removing the bullet closest to his heart, he slipped into a coma."

My heart ached as my son broke down in the middle of the hallway. I knew how close he and his father were. I could only imagine how bad it was tearing him up, but regardless of whether he was ready, it was now his time to take over and pick up where his father and I had left off.

"There's no time for tears, Nitro," I said as I held him up. "Your time is now. Now, carry on in the absence of your father."

"How?" he cried into my shoulder.

"That's the easy part," I replied, forcing him to look at me. "You carry on as if nothing is wrong. You think something like this has never happened before? Well, it has, and you wanna know what your father did?"

"What?"

"He went about as planned. Even when madness is all around you, you never let that fuck with business."

I held my son tightly in my arms. I knew he was hurting. So was I, but I knew what game we'd been playing. I knew the game that we chose. Although it hurt like hell, Willie and I both knew the risks and consequences of our actions. We did it willingly to feed our family.

"Wipe them tears," I instructed. "And go find them motherfuckers and bring them to me."

"Yes, ma'am," he answered.

"And . . ." I called out to him, "we have a leak. Only you, me, and Ace know about your father. So, you must maintain the idea that nothing is wrong and your father is fine. The last thing we need is anyone thinking they have the upper hand on us just because your father is down. I'd hate to resort to my old ways if anything happened to you. So, keep that in mind."

Chapter Twenty-three

Dionne

"I still can't believe that she was shot," I said as Dylan drove down the narrow road that led to Myleena's place. "That shit sound like some straight gangsta movie type of shit."

"Well, I ain't a gangsta type of bitch," Dylan shouted. "Ain't no way in hell I'ma let a bullet wound fuck up this body," he said as he admired himself in his rearview mirror. "I am *definitely* God's gift to the world," he giggled.

"More like God's curse," I joked.

"Bitch, please. You just be sure to keep yo' crazy-ass thoughts to a bare minimum."

"I ain't worried about you or that warning," I spat as we pulled up to Myleena's place. "Besides, she never told us how much fun she had at the party."

"Bitch, please. Now, you know damn well you don't care if she had fun or not. All you care about is knowing if that fine-ass nigga Ace was there with a date."

I sucked my lips at him before a smile appeared. He knew me too damn well. Although I did care about Myleena's well-being, now that I knew she would be okay, I wanted the scoop on Ace. Dylan continued to fuss at me and my nosy-ass ways as we walked up the path to the house. While we approached the door, all I could think about was that bitch LaToya and how she acted whenever we would come over. Knowing that bitch only had a few more times to say some slick shit out of her mouth before I caved her entire face in, I made sure that my shoes were laced and tied.

Dylan knocked on the door as I waited behind him. More than a few minutes had passed since we stood on the porch before the door finally opened. We both smiled as Myleena answered the door, but the worried look on her face told us that something was wrong. As we looked down to see what she was holding, it became apparent that things weren't kosher.

"What's up?" I asked as my eyebrows wrinkled. "Is everything okay?"

With a gun in her hand, Myleena looked around cautiously before inviting us in. My heart dropped at her nervousness. She was usually perky and happy whenever we came around. It didn't take a genius to tell us something was very wrong.

"What's going on?" Dylan and I asked as she sat us down in the living room.

"A lot," she answered in a quivering voice. "I feel like it's all happening again."

"Like what's happening again?" Dylan asked as I quickly took the gun from her hand and placed it on the glass coffee table in front of us.

Dylan and I were floored when Myleena finished telling us everything that had happened within the past few hours. I was from the hood. I knew all about Nitro and the business that his family did in the streets, but what I couldn't figure out was who would want his father dead. They were the most respected family in the hood, but on the other hand, I could. So many corner dope boys in the hood wanted what they had. So many people would kill just to get a taste of the good life. I knew that the so-called good life wasn't all good. I knew that with gold came robbers who wanted to take it from you. I knew that behind every hungry dog, there was an even hungrier dog behind him.

I saw the tears in Myleena's eyes as she told us what was going on, and all I could do was feel sorry for her. She had gone through so much and had lost her entire family before coming to America. Hearing that she thought it was starting to happen all over again and that there wasn't anything she could do to stop it was heartbreaking.

"So, I don't think that it's safe for y'all to be around me anymore," she said, looking from Dylan to me. "I think that the same person who killed my family is trying to do the same thing here. I don't want anything bad to happen to you. I wouldn't be able to live with myself if it did," she said as she broke down.

"Girl, fuck that bullshit," Dylan stated as he sat closer to her. "Like we told you before, we're together on this," he said as he looked at me.

"We're family," I replied as I sat on the other side of her.

We hugged her until the tears finally stopped. I know a hug wasn't much, but it was all she needed, and we were right there to give it to her.

Now, Dylan felt it would be good to change the subject and move away from Myleena's terrible ordeal. He asked about the party, hoping to lighten the mood. It worked.

"Well, we've got some catching up to do," Myleena said, perking up a bit. "I have to tell y'all about the party."

"Yassss!" I clapped. "I been waiting to hear about it."

"Well, it was a lot of fun. Like something you would only see on television, but I was there."

"What about Ace?" I blurted out. "Was he there? Who was he with?"

"Yes. He was there, and he didn't have a date."

"Thank God," I exclaimed.

"Bitch, that still don't mean that he don't have a woman. He could be like most people and want that part of his life to stay private," Dylan said with a roll of his eyes.

"Leave it to Dylan to piss in my cornflakes," I joked.

"Nah, I'm not pissing. I'm just stating that some people like privacy in their private lives."

"I kissed him," Myleena blurted out, causing Dylan and me to look at her in confusion.

"What?" I asked. "Who did you kiss?"

"Nitro."

At first, my heart dropped out of fear that she was telling me she had kissed Ace, but now, my heart was leaping for joy at her kissing Nitro. I knew I wasn't crazy. I could see that they were feeling each other, and his bitch, LaToya, would have been a damn fool if she didn't see it too.

"Oh my God!" I screamed. "I *knew* it! I knew it! I knew it!" I repeated as I jumped up and down.

"Sit yo' ass down. You acting like you the one that got a kiss," Dylan fussed. "Myleena, ignore this sexless ho," he said as he fanned me away. "I've been daydreaming about what it would be like to kiss Nitro Johnson. So, spill the tea, honey. I wanna know all about it."

"Honestly, it was everything I imagined it would be. His lips were so soft. It felt like bolts of electricity were shooting through my body." She blushed. "My dad would kill me. Especially if he knew about the dreams that I've been having about him," she confessed.

"Wait, what? You been having dreams about him?" I asked as I sat my ass back down.

Dylan's thot ass was getting hot in the ass about a kiss. I was more interested in some dick action.

"Yes."

"What kind of dreams?" Dylan asked.

"Wild dreams. Some of him taking his clothes off in front of me. Others of us in the shower. Sometimes, I even wake up, and my sheets are completely soaked," Myleena confessed.

"Oh shit," I yelled. "My baby just had her first sex dream. He must got some fire."

"Don't believe this ho," Dylan said. "Some dream dick will be good as hell, and then when you get the reality dick, it just be so depressing," Dylan said as he placed his hand on his forehead, being his usual dramatic self. "It be more like a suicidal dick," he said before he burst into laughter.

"I ain't never had no dick like that," I spat back.

"I haven't had any at all," Myleena replied quietly.

"Oh damn," I said. "I completely forgot about that. Well, let me be the first to tell you that the first time, it's going to hurt like hell. Not to mention the blood and how much you're gonna be hurting after," I told her. "Especially if he does it right."

"It hurts?" she questioned.

"Only for a minute," I said.

"I don't think I wanna do it," she replied. "Pain?" she questioned.

"Believe me, the ass is worse," I said as I looked at Dylan.

"And, bitch, how the hell would *you* know that?" he asked with sarcasm before turning to Myleena. "Myleena, don't listen to this chick. I'm a pro, and it damn sure didn't hurt my first time."

"Maybe because you was already sticking shit up yo' ass before yo' first time."

"Oh my God! Too much," Myleena laughed.

We continued to laugh and talk to Myleena until the sun went down. We eventually ended up passing out on the floor and couch until the front door burst open. We heard the sounds of heels and keys as the footsteps got closer before the lights were switched on. I looked up from the floor at the Red Bottom stilettos standing before me. It wasn't before long that I was staring up into the glaring eyes of LaToya.

"Where the fuck is Nitro?"

Chapter Twenty-four

LaToya

My blood was boiling once I turned on the lights and saw these motherfuckers as they lay carelessly on the couches that I had imported from France when Nitro first closed on this house. While I've been panicking about what's been going on with Nitro, here these bitches were, being happy and shit. Sleeping like they didn't have a care in the fucking world.

"Where the fuck is Nitro?" I repeated.

"He's not here," Myleena answered as she sat up on the couch. "Is something wrong?" she asked as she looked at the clock on one of the end tables.

"That would be none of your damn business," I spat. "In fact, none of this is your business. So, I suggest that you keep your fucking mouth shut. Didn't your parents ever tell you only to speak when spoken to?" I asked sarcastically.

"Excuse me?" she said.

"You heard what the fuck I said."

"Yeah, but I don't think she should have," her friend said as she jumped up and faced me.

Now standing toe-to-toe with this bitch, I could spit fire. As if I couldn't get any angrier, I closed my eyes as I tried to calm down. Between Bruno hounding me for money and me not knowing how much information Nitro knew about the shooting, especially with me having a hand in all of this, I was slowly but surely driving myself up the fucking wall.

"Look, I don't know who you think I am . . . but I'll tell you who I'm not—" I stated before she cut me off.

"I don't give a fuck who you are, but what you're *not* gonna do is come up in here and disrespect . . . That's a fact—not a threat."

"Who are you to tell me anything?" I asked. "I could make a single phone call and have yo' ass kidnapped and in a body bag in a matter of minutes."

"And for you to make that phone call, you'd have to make it to a phone first," LaToya threatened as she looked at me menacingly. "And trust me, I won't let you make it that far."

"Look, y'all, just chill out," the guy they called Dylan said as he stood between us. "We don't know where Nitro is, but he hasn't come here."

I took deep breaths as I looked at him through narrow eyes. I wanted so badly to smack the taste from his lips, but instead of acting on my thoughts, I placed my keys on the coffee table as I walked around, and my eyes grew wide when they landed on the gun.

"Oh shit," I said. "He knows. He knows something."

"He knows what?" Myleena asked as she stepped toward me. "Is Nitro okay?"

"Bitch, I told you before not to speak to me," I yelled. "I don't know why the fuck Nitro is allowing you to stay here! Especially not with this ghetto bitch you keep around you and especially not with that knockoff RuPaul-looking-ass nigga beside her."

"Oh no, she didn't," Dylan yelled. "I *know* I look better than RuPaul. Dionne, get her ass! Just off principle."

"Say less," Dionne yelled.

Before I knew what was happening, I felt hands as I was pulled backward. I hit the floor with a hard thud before I felt hands rain down on my face. I tried to block as many blows as possible, but everything was happening so fast that my hands and mind couldn't keep up with what was happening.

"Bitch, I told you not to disrespect her again," she said in between blows to my face. "But you didn't want to listen, and then you come for my brother," she yelled.

"Dionne!" I heard Myleena yell. "Stop! Please, stop!"

In between her blows to my face, I could see Myleena and Dylan trying to pull her off of me. Feeling trapped on the ground, I was in flight-or-bite mode! Seeing no other way out of this beat-down, I opened my mouth and bit the closest thing to me.

"Ow! You bitch!" she screamed before I received a kick to my head.

I screamed, cried, and prayed for them to get her off of me. My prayers were soon answered when a big pair of hands lifted her off me and pulled her to the corner. My whole body was aching as I tried to sit up. I was in a daze as I felt something leaking down my face. My head viciously throbbed as I placed my hand near my eyebrow. Tears threatened to fall when I saw my hand covered in blood. Looking over, I was relieved to see Nitro finally. But instead of him seeing about *my* injuries, he was walking over to that bitch Myleena.

"What's going on?" he asked as he looked from me to her.

"Can't you see what's going on?" I asked as I looked at Dionne, who Ace held back. "That bitch attacked me!"

"You just don't learn," she yelled as she tried to break away from Ace's hold. "Let me go!"

"Myleena, what happened?"

With rage but too scared to move, I listened as Myleena told him what had just happened. When she finally stopped talking, Nitro picked up my car keys, walked over to me, and picked me up. Expecting for him to carry me to his bedroom and nurse my wounds, I was confused when he instead walked in the direction of the front door.

"What's going on, Nitro?" I asked as he opened the door. It was dark and raining as he placed me on my feet.

"You need to go."

"But, Nitro," I cried, "that bitch attacked me, and that bitch Myleena just stood there," I screamed as tears streamed down my face.

"I told yo' ass once before never to call her a bitch again," he yelled as he looked behind him over his shoulder. I saw how his scowl turned into a small smile before he looked back at me.

"It's okay, Myleena," he said. "I got this."

My heart was breaking as I saw how he looked at her. His look was so gentle, so calming, so loving. He looked at her in a way that he'd *never* looked at me.

"You love her," I said in amazement.

Instead of answering me, he just shut the door in my face. Feeling hurt and defeated, I walked down the steps. The rain pounded my body, and my hair hung low and dripped as I walked to my car. I no longer cared about the rain, getting wet, or even getting sick. My life was ending. My man—my meal ticket—was gone.

I sat in my car and stared up at the house. I helped him pick this house. I helped him decorate it. I helped him do it all, and now, this bitch was reaping the benefits from all of *my* hard work. I cried as I thought of how my life was spiraling out of control. How was I going to live without Nitro? How was I going to pay all my bills? How was I going to live the life that I deserved without him?

Those thoughts plagued my mind as I drove down the streets of Manhattan. That sadness and lost feeling soon turned into rage and bitterness. If he thought that I was just gonna let him dump me and that be the end of it, he had another think coming.

"If you think that it's over, Nitro, you're crazier than me," I said as I felt myself unlock a new level of insanity.

If he thought that I was only capable of calling a few bitches with a few fake pregnancies, then he had no idea what I was *truly* capable of. He had no idea who I *really* was. He had no idea how miserable I'd make him, and he had no idea of how miserable I could make that bitch. At that moment, I made a vow to myself. I would claim what was rightfully mine and the lives of those who tried to take it from me.

Chapter Twenty-five

Myleena

"I apologize for that," I said once Nitro walked back into the living room. "I didn't mean for none of that to happen."

"No need to apologize," he replied, caressing my cheek and looking at Dionne. "I'm sure she said some shit to make her deserve the ass whooping that she got."

"That ain't even the word for it," Dionne spat as she walked away from Ace and over to me. "Are you okay?"

"I'm fine," I replied. "Thanks for that," I said, referring to her stepping up for me.

"No problem. I told you, you are family."

"Well, if the royal rumble is over, it's getting late, and my baby is calling me for some late-night sugar," Dylan said, causing all of us to look at him.

"What about my ride home?" Dionne asked with her hands on her hips.

"I'll take you," Ace spoke up.

My eyes shot open in surprise as I looked at Dionne's nervous but excited look. Dylan winked at us both before he made his way out the door. I walked over to Dionne as Ace and Nitro walked toward his office.

"Oh my God," she squealed, jumping up and down.

"This is your chance," I said, joining in on her excitement. I knew how much she liked Ace, and although we had no idea if he had a girlfriend, we figured this would be her chance to find out.

"What do I do?" she asked nervously. "What do I say? Do I talk to him, or should I be quiet?"

"Stop worrying about all of that," I said in a hushed tone. "Just be yourself."

"What if he don't like me?"

"Well then, that'll just be his loss," I answered as Nitro and Ace reappeared from the back of the house.

"Are you ready?" he asked as he looked at her.

"Yes," she replied. "Thanks again."

"No problem at all."

I gave Dionne one last smile before she got into Ace's car, and they drove down the road. The thunder roared as I turned around to the door to see Nitro looking at me with a smile, which caused me to smile. I don't know what it was about him, but something about his smile made my heart flutter. His smile was comforting.

"Come on in the house before you get soaked."

I smiled as I followed him into the house. Then I looked around at the mess that the fight between Dionne and LaToya had left. I hummed a tune as I tidied up the living room. The feeling of someone staring at me caused me to turn around. I slightly jumped when I saw Nitro staring silently at me in the middle of the doorway.

"What?" I asked as I took a seat on the couch.

"Nothing," he answered as he sat beside me. "Just thinking."

"What are you thinking about?" Then I remember how much of a rush he was in earlier after receiving that phone call.

"Everything."

"What was that phone call about?" I asked. "The one that made you rush out of the house. Is everything okay?"

Sadness filled his eyes as he glanced down at the floor. His sudden mood change made my heart race.

"What is it?" I asked as I forced him to look at me.

"Can I trust you?" he asked.

"Of course, you can."

It felt like an eternity had passed, with us staring at each other. As I stared into his eyes, I wished that I could take away whatever pain he was hiding.

"My father was shot today."

My heart raced, and my mind zoned out as I had a flashback of when I was shot. It was so painful. There was so much blood. It was something that I never wanted to experience again.

"I'm so sorry," I said, wrapping my arms around him. "Is he going to be okay?"

"They were able to remove the bullets, but as they tried to remove the last one next to his heart, he slipped into a coma."

As I held him in my arms, I heard the silent sniffling of him crying. I hugged him tightly. The same way he did me so many times in the past.

"It's going to be okay, Nitro. I'm here for you," I whispered.

I caressed his back until the tears stopped. He finally looked up at me. His eyes were bloodshot, and his face drew closer to mine. I closed my eyes as our lips touched. I felt that spark again. That same spark that shot through me the night of his mother's party. The same shock I wanted to shoot through me for the rest of my life.

I moaned into him as he laid me back on the couch and slithered like a snake between my legs. I wrapped my arms around his neck when his hands slowly roamed up my body as his tongue swirled with mine. His gentle caressing soon turned into a rough squeeze and felt like a fire had exploded in my body; I liked it. I liked it more than I should have. I liked it even though I knew it was wrong.

Somewhere in between our kissing, his shirt disappeared. I glanced down and instantly saw the tattoos that covered his body. The same tattooed body that I had been dreaming about for weeks. I would see the same tattoos when he was working out at his home gym. The same tattoos that would often make my mouth water. My eyes shot up in shock when I felt him poking me through my thin sweatpants. The words of Dionne echoed through my head at how painful it would be to have sex for the first time.

"Mmm," I moaned. "Nitro, stop."

I quickly felt him as he rose from my body and stared at me. His eyes were so beautiful as they glimmered under the dim light.

"What's wrong?" he asked. "I didn't hurt you, did I?"

"No. It's just that . . . I can't . . ." I stuttered. "I can't do this."

"Damn," he mumbled to himself. "I'm sorry about that."

"It's okay," I replied. "I want to. I just don't know if it's the right thing to do."

"It's okay. You don't have to explain. I understand."

My nerves were all over the place as I looked at him. I could feel my private area throbbing from excitement. As much as I wanted to be with him, I couldn't. Nitro smiled at me as he stood up from the couch. I wanted to talk to him. I felt the need to tell him my reasons for making him stop. It was no longer fear of dishonoring my family because I no longer had one. My reason was fear, fear of the pain from making love for the first time.

"I'ma go to bed. Call me if you need anything," he said as he walked down the hall. "I'll see you in the morning."

I could finally breathe again once I heard the door to his bedroom close. My heart was racing as I thought of what had just happened. I closed my eyes and savored the taste of his tongue as it was still fresh on my lips. Getting up, I walked into my bedroom and closed the door. I lay on my bed and stared at the ceiling before closing my eyes.

I pictured Nitro lying on top of me while softly caressing my body as he did moments ago. I imagined my hands as his as they traveled below my waist and reached inside my panties. Although I knew what I was doing was wrong, I didn't care. It felt good. It made me feel as if I weren't alone. It made me feel loved. I played with my love button as I imagined that he would.

"Aah," I moaned as I closed my eyes tight.

I gently rubbed on my clit in a slow, circular motion before gently inserting one of my fingers inside myself. I thrust my finger in and out continuously until my legs shook. My breathing quickened as I felt a sensation build in the lowest part of my stomach.

"Aah," I moaned again as I squeezed my legs tightly together when I felt myself explode from the inside to the outside.

I was seeing stars, and I enjoyed the feeling that now rested in my belly as my legs still slightly tingled. My smile was big and bright as I opened my eyes and walked to the bathroom. I turned on the shower and allowed the steam from the hot water to fill the bathroom. Then I pulled my hair out of the ponytail and allowed it to hang down my back before I stepped into the shower.

The feeling of the hot water as it cascaded down my body only enhanced the feeling of the orgasm that I had just had. As I washed myself, I again pictured my hands as Nitro's. I imagined his hands as they brushed against my private areas.

"If only it would really happen," I mumbled.

Chapter Twenty-six

Ace

The car ride was silent as the radio played low while I drove down Main Street. Dionne's frequent staring at me caused me to smirk as I looked back at her. I couldn't stand the awkward silence, so I decided to break the ice.

"So, what was the fight about?" I asked casually.

"What?" she asked as she turned to look at me.

"The fight between you and LaToya. What was it about? Don't get me wrong. I dislike her just as much as you do, so I won't judge, but for real, what was it about?"

I could see her looking at me as the streetlights whizzed by her head. Her light brown eyes sparkled under each streetlight that we passed. There was a brief pause in our conversation as she stared out the window at the passing street signs.

"It was about Myleena. I'm tired of the way that LaToya treats her. Myleena does nothing to her, but every chance LaToya gets, she takes jabs at her. Myleena has been through too much shit to have to put up with hers. I'm tired of her thinking that she can disrespect people and think it's okay."

"What about your other friend?" I asked. "The guy."

"Dylan," she corrected me. "His name is Dylan, and he is more than just a guy. He's my best friend. He's like a brother to me. Her disrespecting me or Myleena was one thing. When she disrespected Dylan, she crossed the line."

"I assumed that you two are close."

"Yes. He's always been there for me when I wanted and needed him. He doesn't judge me for how I act or think. He shows me that he really loves me for me, so I show him that same love and loyalty. So, the fact that LaToya thought that it was okay to disrespect him is *not* cool. He's been through so much. As a kid, he's spent so many years being afraid to be himself out of fear of what people would say about him or do to him because they don't understand or choose not to accept him. He spent too many years for him to feel bad now or to let anyone try to down him. I refuse to allow it to happen. Not in front of me."

I could see that just her talking about the subject was getting her upset. Deciding not to upset her any further, I dropped the subject. A few more minutes of silence passed. But her frequent glances at me only told me that there was something that she wanted to say, something that she wanted to ask.

"Is something wrong?" I asked.

"No," she stuttered. "I was just wondering . . ."

"Wondering what?"

"Wondering what you do for Myleena and Nitro."

"You're asking that, but I'm sure you already know," I replied. "If you need me to tell you, I'm their bodyguard," I said with a laugh.

"What's so funny?"

"You," I answered. "You think I don't see you. I see you all the time watching me. Which tells me that you know exactly what I do."

I smiled as her cheeks turned red from embarrassment. I busted her for her fake ignorance. Just like she was secretly watching me all those times, I was watching her too—watching her and waiting to make my move.

"So," I said as we approached a red light, "what's your story?"

"What do you mean?"

"What are you going to school for? What are your plans? Goals? Are you single?"

"I'm going to school to become a lawyer. I want to make a difference. Dylan always told me that my mouth could back people into a corner. So, I decided, why not use the gift that God gave me?"

"I feel that," I replied with a nod. "What about your future?"

"Me being a lawyer *is* my future," she giggled.

Now I felt embarrassed for not realizing that I had asked her the same question twice. With those two questions answered, there was only one question left.

"Are you single?" I asked.

"What?" she asked, stunned as if she didn't hear me the first time.

"You heard me. I asked if you were single."

"Yes," she answered.

"Why is that?"

"What do you mean, why?"

"I mean, you're beautiful, talented, loyal, and got a good head on your shoulders. If what you're telling me is the truth, I don't understand why you're single."

"Honestly, time," she replied with a shrug. "Life is too short to waste it, and the last thing I want to do is waste time on a man who means me no good. Not to mention, I'm scared of getting my heart broken."

I could only agree with her words. I too understood and knew how valuable and priceless time was. With my job in the streets, I knew every day wasn't promised. And with the war that was brewing, it only confirmed it.

"What about you?" she asked as we pulled into her apartment complex. "Why are *you* single?"

I looked out my window at the corner boys who ran back and forth to the corner. I pondered over her question as they made serve after serve. I looked back at Dionne. Her light brown eyes shimmered as her skin glowed under the streetlights.

"Pretty much the same as you. Time is too short to waste any of it. So, I'd rather be alone."

"But that's no way to live. Everyone desires to be loved."

"Not with the life I live in these streets," I countered.

"Even beasts need peace. Why not try to find a woman who can be your peace?"

"What woman you know would be okay with a nigga who's not promised to come home every day? Who must constantly watch his back and dodge bullets? That's no way to live, but I know that it's the life I chose."

"I would," she answered after gazing at me. "As long as I know you're for me at the end of the day."

Chapter Twenty-seven

Unknown

Two Days Later

I sat in the back of the strip club as Beast and Bone danced behind two bitches. On a regular day, I might have been in my feelings about how touchy Beast was being. Not anymore. I was no longer that bitch in love. I was no longer a bitch with a heart. I was a bitch with a plan, and I knew that for my plan to work, I had to play my part. I had to play the part of the main chick of a boss nigga.

"Wassup, boss lady?" Courtney said as she sat beside me.

"Nothing much," I answered, eying the dark chocolate beauty next to me.

I couldn't help but play with my tongue as I admired her beauty. Courtney used to be just a female with whom Beast and I have had threesomes on occasion, but ever since Beast's coming out party, it was less of us three and more of just us two. How her gray contacts complemented her smooth, dark skin was beyond mesmerizing. Her thick and naturally curly hair perfectly framed her face and made her look like she could be a model for *Jet* magazine. My eyes danced as they traveled her thick frame with ample breasts and a thin waist attached to a perfectly round ass that I used to love to see bouncing up and down on Beast's dick. She smiled as she caught my gaze.

"You like what you see?" she asked with a wink.

"You know I do."

"Well, what are you gonna do about it?" she asked seductively.

I kept my eyes on her as I slid closer. She threw her head back in ecstasy as I slid my hand up her black minidress while my other hand gently massaged her breast. I felt her chest as it heaved up and down as I gently bit and sucked on her neck. Since I no longer wanted affection from Beast, he drove me right into the arms of Courtney. We spent so much time together that I knew her body inside and out. I knew exactly what buttons to play with and how hard to bite to push her over the edge.

"That feels so good," she moaned loudly as she squeezed her legs tightly around my arm. "But not right here. People are watching."

"You think I give a fuck?" I asked through clenched teeth.

"I know you don't," she giggled. "But me?"

A wicked smile graced my face as I looked around the club. Beast and Bone were too busy keeping up their heterosexual front to be watching me and what I was doing. I stopped in the middle of sucking her neck just to look at her. Once upon a time, I would have never even dreamed that I would be attracted to another woman, not to mention fuck them, but as I looked into Courtney's eyes and as her lust dripped down my fingers, I wanted her. I wanted her in every way that I could have her.

"Fine," I replied with a smile. "Meet me in the bathroom," I said before I got up and walked away.

Beast and I now locked eyes, but I didn't care. If he was gonna eat his cake, I was damn sure gonna help myself to a few slices of my own. People danced to the beat of the music and blew their rent money on the strippers as Courtney and I made our way to the bathroom. She wrapped her arms tightly around my waist as we opened the door and walked to the biggest stall. I wasted no time placing her leg on the edge of the toilet and slipping her dress above her hips.

She moaned as she leaned her body against the wall. I smirked as I slipped her panties to the side and dove into that ocean she called a pussy. I slurped and swirled my tongue around her pussy as she pushed my head deeper.

"Damn, B," she moaned as her grip on my hair got tighter. "You're a lot better than Beast."

Just the thought of Beast and the way he let Bone fuck him in the ass pissed me off and made my tongue go faster. I drove it deeper and faster into her as I tried to push the thoughts of Beast and Bone from my mind. I kept my eyes on her as she rotated her hips to match the thrusts of my tongue.

"Right there," she screamed as she gripped the stall to kccp her balance.

Already knowing just what it took to push her over the edge, I smiled as I inserted one finger inside her and used my thumb to massage her clit. Within seconds, her juices were running down her legs. Feeling victorious, I smiled as she got herself together.

"Thanks," she said as she licked the sides of my mouth. "Thanks for giving me something I never knew I needed."

"I think I enjoyed it more than you did," I replied as I stuck my tongue down her throat.

"Don't you always?" she asked sarcastically.

"You never disappoint," I smiled.

She giggled like a schoolgirl as I walked over to the sink. I took out the small bottle of mouthwash that I kept in my purse for occasions such as this. I gargled the minty liquid as I looked at Courtney, and she looked at me with lust.

"What?" I asked.

"I want some of you," she answered as she reached around and gripped my pussy. "I miss the taste of *that*."

"Then be waiting for me at your place when I leave here," I instructed before turning around. "I'll give you all you want for as long as you want."

"What about Beast? Are you willing to let him find out about us?" she asked. "I know about him and Bone. You deserve so much better, B, which is why you deserve to be mines."

"Don't worry about Beast. I'll take care of that. Until that time comes, be patient and know I got you."

I knew Courtney was beginning to catch feelings for me like I was about her. What was once a "make me cum, and afterward, go on about your business" arrangement was now me staying to cuddle and talk after we fucked each other's brains out. Besides Beast, Courtney was now the only person that I trusted with my life. After walking out the door, I walked right into Bone. I looked up at him as he stared at me with knowing eyes.

"Beast is looking for you."

"If he wanted me, I'm sure he would've found me," I spat as I walked back to the VIP section.

I immediately saw him as he sat at one of the tables with some big-booty bitch shaking her ass in his face. I couldn't help but shake my head as she turned to face him. I laughed as she showed him her titties. Butch bitch looked like Mark Henry in a scuba suit.

"If only you knew," I said to myself as I approached him.

"Where you been?" he asked as his eyes landed on me.

"Around," I answered while looking around the club. Then I saw Courtney as she approached the exit before briefly looking in my direction.

After ensuring she had made it safely out of the club, I turned my attention back to Beast. Just as I stared at him, I looked at the stripper. She would have been a cute girl if it were not for her having a giant mole hanging off her chin, but at a strip club, I knew that the faces on these bitches were irrelevant if their bodies were on point. I laughed at her as she looked at me as if she were proud that she had my man's attention. Truth be told, I knew the *real* him, while she only knew the man that he portrayed to be in public.

"Around where? I haven't seen you in about twenty minutes."

Just from his vibe and demeanor, I could tell that he was irritated. How his jaws flexed each time he spoke told me he wasn't in a happy mood. His not being in a happy mood would be an absolute hell for me later.

"Let's go," he demanded as he got up abruptly, damn near causing the girl who was once dancing in front of him to fall on her ass.

She looked so embarrassed as she glanced around the partially filled section but quickly recovered as she looked for another booth. She was probably looking for her next prey for the night. I shook my head as I turned around and followed Beast. Walking toward the stairs, I stumbled into a solid frame.

"Whoa!" he said as he grabbed me by the waist. "You good?" he asked.

For the first time in a long time, as I looked up, I saw a man who would've made a puddle in any woman's panties, from his brown eyes to his crisp haircut. The strength in his arms as they held me and stopped me from falling on my ass told me that he worked out on a regular because I was far from a skinny bitch. I was what most niggas called a slim, thick bitch. I looked from him to the dreadhead who stood right behind him and was just as handsome. Hell, if I could've had them both, I would.

Seeing Beast behind them both snapped me from my thoughts as I remembered who and where I was.

"Yeah, I'm good," I replied, sidestepping them and following Beast out of the club.

Although my legs were following Beast, my thoughts were still on the sexy gentleman that I had just bumped into.

"You have a good time tonight?" Beast asked as we pulled out of the parking lot.

"I sure did."

"So, that's the game you wanna play," he asked, "disappearing with Courtney for as long as you did?"

"I only play the game that's being played," I answered as I texted Courtney. "So, are you sure these are the games *you* wanna play?"

"A'ight, B, don't let that bitch be the reason that you end up six feet deep," he threatened as he clutched the steering wheel.

I paid his ass no mind as my phone alerted me to a text message. I smirked when she told me that she was on her way home. Just as much as she missed the taste of me, I missed the taste of her too. I was a fiend, and I needed my fix. Don't get me wrong. I've had my fair share of pussy, but hers tasted so much sweeter. I tuned out Beast and his bitching as I thought about how good my night was and how it was about to get even better.

Here I come, baby, I thought as I side eyed the complete waste of a man sitting beside me.

Chapter Twenty-eight

Nitro

I sat in the back of the club while the rest of my niggas popped bottles and made it rain on the strippers, but as my boys threw money at them, all I could think about was the woman who bumped into me on my way up here. I had only gotten a quick look at her. I'd be lying if I said that she wasn't beautiful. Just as she was beautiful, though, there was something so familiar about her eyes. It was almost as if I had already met her, but I just couldn't place where.

My mind was completely gone as the celebration went on around me. Although I was out with my boys, I was in my own head about my current situation. My father was in a coma, fighting for his life, and my mother worried if he would make it. On top of that, LaToya was bombarding me with calls. I was getting at least thirty phone calls from her daily. When I wouldn't answer, she sent voicemails stating how much she loved me and wanted to be with me to her now saying fuck me and everything that I stood for. Most men would find the shit comical, but I knew how critical a scorned woman could be.

So, I was sure to hit her back, saying we were good, at least for now. She was still on my radar about the shooting that happened at my mother's party, especially after how happy her tone was when she asked about making funeral arrangements for Myleena once I told her that she was shot. As I thought more about it, I hated the fact that we still didn't have a lead on the main nigga who was responsible for shooting Myleena on the night of the party.

Luckily for me, a few weeks after the shooting, the streets started talking and gave up a few of the niggas who were behind it. Although we killed the niggas that pulled the triggers, we still had no clue who was pulling the strings and calling the shots. The fact that them niggas said that they'd rather die before they snitched on who it was only pissed me off more. As much as I wanted to be combing the streets for answers, I couldn't let down my crew by missing this special night. As my mom said, the last thing we needed to do was to let the streets know that the head of our empire was in a coma. That would only give whoever these niggas were more ammunition to come at us with full clips because they thought we were injured.

We were out celebrating the chance to make money—more money in a week than we'd ever made when my dad was in charge. With our new connect came new custom-ers, and new customers adding to our old customers only meant one thing . . . more money. My mother told me to follow two rules, even while my father was down. The first rule was to continue to make boss and business moves for the good of the family, no matter the circumstances. There were times when my dad would be planning funer-als for his top soldiers, but he never let that deter him from making his money. The second rule was never to let the streets see you sweat.

That rule alone was the reason that I made it my mis-sion to be seen popping bottles and making it rain on the bitches surrounding me, even if my mind wasn't there. While making more money was a celebration for me, with the life that most of my crew lived, every day was a celebration for them—the celebration of living another day, a celebration of being able to feed their families, another day of being a member on a winning team.

"Ayo, Nitro!" my right-hand man and best friend since childhood called out to me. "Where you at, nigga?" he asked with a bottle of champagne in one hand and a stripper's ass in the other.

"I'm here," I lied while shaking the thoughts from my head.

"Are you sure?" Ace asked sarcastically. One thing about Ace was that he knew me. In fact, he knew me almost better than I knew myself. So, he knew when I was lying.

"What?"

"Man, you just had one of the baddest strippers that this club had to offer in yo' lap, and you barely even looked at her."

I couldn't help but shake my head again and laugh at Ace as he now had girls with their hands all over him. Since we were kids, he's always prided himself on being a ladies' man. He was the only nigga that I knew who lost his virginity when he was 10 years old. The real kicker to the story is the fact that he lost his virginity to our math teacher, who was also the mother of the girl he was dating at the time.

"This y'all scene," I laughed. "Not mine."

"That's right," he replied sarcastically. "You'd rather be at home playing chess with LaToya yelling at you in the background," he laughed. "I don't see the point in that damn game anyway."

"Some see it as a pointless game, but in the game we're in, it's a way to see all angles of possible targets and all areas of weakness," I replied as I thought back to the day I said the same thing to my father.

In fact, after that long conversation with my father, I never looked at that game the same way ever again. Damn was all that I could say as I thought of how badly I allowed myself to fall off. The fact that my father had to suffer for it only made my conscience grow worse.

"I'm out," I said to Ace as I stood up from the booth.

"You calling it a night?"

"Yeah. I'll cover y'all niggas' tab. I'll check wit'chu tomorrow."

"Bet," he called out over the music.

I nodded to a few of the fellas as I made my way out of the club and to my car. My gun rested on my lap as I weaved in and out of traffic. The wind of the mid-December air was all that could be heard through the car as I pulled up to my place. I took the time to look up at my house . . . a home I had built from the ground up that cost me a pretty penny to create.

I took a deep breath, took my keys out of the ignition, and got out of the car. The wind blew past my face as I walked up the stairs. The fragrance of Zen invaded my nose as soon as I stepped inside. That smell alone told me that I was home, the one place where I felt safe.

I looked at the pictures of my father and me as I walked down the hall. The hall led me to the living room, where I flopped down on the sofa. For the first time in a long time, I felt helpless as I sat alone with my thoughts. So many thoughts flooded my mind. Thoughts about my father lying up in a hospital bed, fighting for his life. Thoughts of my mother and how she must be feeling knowing that at any given moment, the love of her life could slip away. Somewhere in between my thoughts, a tear dropped from my eye. One tear turned into two, and soon, those two turned into many more.

Just the thought of losing my father was enough to break me down. Even though I knew that he wasn't going to live forever, I just never imagined him being taken away from me like this. Not here, not right now. There were still so many things about the game, being a man, and life that I didn't know yet. If he left me, who would teach it to me?

"Are you okay?"

Looking up, I was somewhat relieved when my dark brown eyes landed on a pair of gray eyes. A weak smile spread across my face as she sat next to me. The sweet scent of her perfume made me want her even closer to me. Something about her tone and presence was so comforting to me.

"I will be," I replied in a low voice. "What are you doing up so late?"

"I always stay up late," she whispered. "I always stay up to be sure that you come in safely," she said as she placed her hand on mine. "I want to make sure that you're okay."

There it was. The same bolt of electricity that I felt the night of my mother's party; the same bolt of electricity that I felt the night that we kissed each other again before she stopped us. That same feeling that I felt that night when I saw her walk down the stairs in that dress for the first time. Her eyes and skin were glowing under the dim lights. Her hair flowed perfectly down her back and rested partially on her shoulders.

"I'm okay," I replied.

"Are you sure?"

I wanted so desperately to tell her how I felt. To tell her how lost I was feeling. To tell her that I needed her. But just as badly as I wanted to say those words, my lips refused to move.

"Okay," she replied as she tried to get up from the sofa before I grabbed her by her arm. The moonlight shining from the window made her eyes sparkle. She looked so beautiful. The way her eyes shimmered gave her a wild edge, almost animalistic. Just as her eyes made her look wild, her face and personality made her so gentle, so calming.

"I don't want to be alone tonight," I found myself saying before I could stop.

From the look in her eyes, I instantly regretted those words as soon as they fell from my mouth.

"You don't have to be," she replied while sitting beside me.

I kept my eyes on her as our faces got closer and closer together. I didn't know about her, but my heart was racing. As our lips touched, I felt something that I'd never felt with anyone. Something that I've never felt about anyone, not even LaToya. Although I wasn't sure what it was, I was ready and willing to do whatever it took to find out.

I took her by the hand as we both rose from the couch. Her grip tightened as I led the way to my bedroom.

"Nitro," she whispered as I laid her gently on the bed.

Chapter Twenty-nine

Myleena

I couldn't believe what I was doing as Nitro lay on top of me. My body felt as if it were on fire as his tongue invaded my mouth and his hands roamed my body. My mind was racing a mile a minute as I thought of the many times I had dreamed of him doing these exact things to me. In the back of my mind, I knew it was wrong, but it felt so right, almost as if it were meant to be.

I closed my eyes as I felt his hands caress my breasts through the fabric of my bra. Within moments, the clasp was snapped, and my breasts were freed. His hands felt so good against my skin. They weren't too rough or too soft. They were perfect as he stripped me out of the rest of my clothing before I helped him out of his. His body had a heavenly glow to it as the flames from the fireplace flickered in the distance.

Upon opening my eyes, I stared deep into his eyes as my hands ran down his inked-up arms. As I looked at him, I suddenly felt nervous, a feeling that I didn't have in any of my fantasies as he stared at me. In my many fantasies, I was always confident in my next moves. Right now, in reality, I wasn't sure what to do. My hair was in disarray as it covered his pillows. His sudden stop of movements caused me to look at him in confusion.

"What's wrong?" I asked, suddenly feeling the need to cover my body.

A smile broke on his face as he took my hands away from my breasts and placed them flat above my head. He kept his eyes on me as he leaned down and put each of my breasts into his mouth before licking the tip of my nipples with his tongue. The feeling that it had on my body was indescribable. It was a mixture of a slight tickle and a tingling sensation that shot down to my most private areas, which only made me shiver from his touch.

"Don't ever cover yourself when you're with me. Nothing is wrong," he answered with a smile before leaning back down to kiss my lips. "You just look so beautiful."

I smiled as I felt my heart flutter. I pushed all the negative thoughts of this being wrong to the back of my mind as I opened my legs to him. I wanted him. At this moment, I felt like I needed him just as much as he needed me.

"Are you sure you want to do this?" he asked.

"I'm sure," I smiled.

I closed my eyes as he leaned into me. I ignored all negative thoughts that tried to creep back into my head as I wrapped my arms around his neck and my legs around his waist. I moaned loudly as he licked, sucked, and placed kisses on my collarbone. His hands sent electric shock waves down my spine as he traveled south, placing more kisses down my body. He stopped just above my waist as he put my legs on the top of his shoulders. I looked down at him as he gently kissed the inside of both of my thighs.

Once again, fear set in. The fear of pain from what I wanted to be a pleasure. Fear of him hurting me, not just my body, but my heart.

"Nitro," I moaned as I tried to focus on him. "Please don't hurt me," I begged.

"Just relax. I promise to be gentle."

Not even a second later, I felt his tongue as it glided across my pearl before entering me. I felt my legs tighten around his neck as I felt him spread my lips apart before sticking his tongue in me as deep as it could go.

"Oooh!" I moaned as I gripped the sheets.

Stars clouded my vision as my back began to arch faster as his tongue flicked across my clit. He quickly developed a routine of rotation as he went from sucking my clit to slurping all of my juices as they began to travel down my body. I placed my hands on his head as he placed both of his hands under my butt and thrust me harder and faster toward his mouth.

My toes curled as I felt a feeling building up in the lowest pit of my stomach. My moans got louder, and my thighs tightened as my legs began to shake uncontrollably. I felt Nitro's fingers as they glided up my body and gently pinched my nipples.

"Aah," I moaned as I gripped the sheets with all my strength.

The strength I once had was now a thing of the past as I felt it run out of me and into his mouth. Looking down at him, I was more than surprised to see his eyes focused on me. He never broke eye contact with me as he traveled back up my body and kissed me. Something about his kiss had me gone. Something about the passionate yet aggressive way that he took my lips into his had me wanting more. As our tongues danced to a rhythm that only they knew the tune to, I could still feel myself throbbing as Nitro rested between my legs.

He gently stroked my hair as he stared into my eyes. Initially, I was afraid, but now, I felt as if I were ready. Suddenly, like so many times in my dreams, I smiled as I crawled on top of him. I knew I was taking a huge leap of faith as I made the first move to kiss him. Like so many times in my fantasy, he kissed me back. At first, it was gentle, but soon, it became more aggressive and with more passion than it was before. It was as if our hearts were desperately trying to get to each other, and our bodies were the pathways to do it.

"Make love to me," I moaned out in between our kisses.

I enjoyed the feeling of having my body pressed so closely against his. I moaned as his hands became tangled in my hair, and our kissing continued. Kisses traveled from my lips and down to my neck as he pulled my head backward by my hair. Although his aggression caused a bit of discomfort, at the same time, it kept me on the edge and begging for more. Soon, the only thing that could be heard throughout the room was the sounds of our lips as they made love.

Our kissing intensified as he put me on my back, and I once again felt the throbbing between my legs. Nitro placed my legs back around his waist as I grinded myself against him. I felt him as he put his rod against my opening. Glancing down, I saw how blessed he was in the men's department, and I instantly became frightened.

"Relax," he replied as if he could read my mind and sense my fear. He leaned down and kissed me on the lips once more. "I won't hurt you."

I took a deep breath as I tried my best to relax. My body tensed as he slid himself into me. With just a few slow and steady strokes, he was in. It may have felt good to him, but it felt like he had utterly broken me in two.

I wrapped my arms tightly around his neck as he slowly thrust himself inside of me. The pain was beyond unbearable as I now gripped his shoulders. I could feel myself as I dug my nails into his skin and dragged them down the sides of his arms. Instead of him stopping from the pain that I was causing him, it seemed to make him go harder.

"Aah!" I moaned as that pain soon turned into pleasure.

My breathing became short and shallow as my legs began to shake. The feeling of his thrusts mixed with the flicking of his tongue as he sucked on my neck was more than enough to send me over the edge.

"I love you," I moaned out as I looked him in his eyes.

We made love for what seemed like hours before I felt him as he throbbed inside of me. His thrusts, which started out long and powerful, soon became short and more rugged. Within minutes, I once again felt myself explode from the inside out. My chest heaved up and down as Nitro glanced down at me with a smile before getting up and walking into his bathroom. Minutes later, I heard the sound of water running.

Looking down, a wave of embarrassment washed over me at the sight of me lying in a puddle of blood.

"Oh my God," I said in shock, covering my mouth with my hand.

My body was sore as I struggled to sit up. I looked around the room for something to cover the stain but found nothing. Realizing that I spoke three fatal words to him as I gave him my body now came rushing to my mind. Looking around the room, the weight of guilt fell on my shoulders, and tears came to my eyes.

"I love him," I repeated, still in shock and disbelief. "And he doesn't even love me back. What have I done?"

Thoughts of my father and mother came to mind as tears spilled from my eyes. I suddenly realized that I had just made the biggest mistake of my life. My father would have had my head if he were still alive. I was so wrapped in my thoughts that I never heard Nitro as he walked back out of the bathroom and approached me. I quickly wiped away the tears as a weak smile came across my face when he stared at me through the fire's dim light.

No words were spoken between us as he picked me up and carried me into his bathroom. I was surprised he had made me a warm bath surrounded by candles.

"This should help with the soreness," he said as he slowly placed me into the bubble-filled tub. "You soak right here. I'll go and change the sheets."

"Oh my God," I said as I held my head down in embarrassment. "I'm so sorry. I ruined your sheets."

"No need for any of that. That's the best memory I've ever had in those sheets," he replied with a chuckle as he walked out of the bathroom.

I silently cried as I thought about what had just taken place. Not just my actions but the ending results as well. I could only shake my head at myself as I thought more about what I had done. Acting on emotions instead of thinking with my head, I was now in the same situation my sister was in years ago. The same situation that had her disowned by our entire family and country. The same situation that had forever labeled her as a whore. That same situation was the reason why I never saw her again.

These thoughts panicked me as I wondered what was going to happen next. I knew that Nitro didn't love me. How could he? He had LaToya. Even though I thought he was too good for her, that didn't mean I was good enough for him, either.

Minutes later, Nitro returned to the bathroom. Wearing a pair of his basketball shorts, he stared at me as he sat on the toilet. He looked at me before grabbing a brush and brushing my hair. I was trapped in my thoughts as Nitro worked.

"I love you too," he whispered, causing me to turn around to face him.

"You do?"

"I do."

His words echoed in my head as he washed my body. Questions plagued my mind as I sat in the tub. Was he honest? Did he *really* love me? Or was he only telling me what I wanted to hear?

"Don't doubt me," he said, picking me up from the tub and drying me off. "I truly do love you."

"How can you love me when you're with LaToya?" I questioned. "It's impossible to be in love with two people simultaneously."

"And I'm not. I've never said those words to LaToya. To be honest, I've never said those words to anyone."

"Then how can you be sure that you love me?"

"The way you make me feel and care for me more than yourself. The way you put your own bullshit to the side just to be there for me when I need you the most. But mostly because I've never been with someone who could make my heart beat faster *and* slower at the same time," he confessed.

There was something so genuine about his words. Even though it could still be a game, I took his word for it. I smiled at him as he kissed my wet lips. Some would probably call me naïve, but I believed his words. I trusted him. We stared into each other's eyes for what felt like forever. This was a perfect moment. I would stay in this moment for the rest of my life if possible.

I was on cloud nine as he picked me up and carried me back into his bedroom. With fresh, clean sheets on his bed, I crawled over to one side of the bed. I closed my eyes as I basked in the memory of being with Nitro. My heart raced, and a smile came to my face as Nitro wrapped his arms tightly around me. I was the happiest I had been in months as I lay in his arms. The feeling of being loved was all that I ever wanted. That feeling alone was all that I could think about as I drifted off into a blissful slumber.

***

The sound of someone banging on the door jolted me from my sleep, causing me to look around in fear. The rays from the sunlight shined brightly through the cream-colored curtains as I remembered everything from the previous night. I smiled as I looked over to the right of me. Looking as beautiful as ever, I looked at Nitro as he lay so peacefully. Other than the constant knocking, the soft sounds of him snoring were the only things that could be heard.

"Nitro," I said as I lightly nudged him. "Nitro," I repeated. This time, he opened his eyes.

"Good morning," he said as he kissed me on the cheek. "How are you feeling?"

"Someone is at the door."

Getting up, he too looked around before glancing at his phone. A look of regret soon covered his face as he looked from his phone to me.

"It's LaToya," he said as he rose from the bed and headed toward the door. "Stay here. I'll be right back."

Chapter Thirty

LaToya

The sun was beaming down on my bare back and making me sweat as I stood on Nitro's front porch. I was fuming as I continued to bang on his door. I looked at my watch. It was well past ten o'clock in the morning, and seeing that all of his cars were parked in his driveway only confirmed that he was home. And I also knew that this was when Nitro left to handle business, which only made me wonder what the hell was keeping him. And not even his lazy-ass maid saw fit to bring her ass down to answer the door only further pissed me off.

I was relentless about seeing him. I didn't care if he was still mad about the hell that I had been causing him lately. He was going to see me and hear what I had to say. After what seemed twenty minutes later, the door finally swung open. I was more than prepared to give whoever opened the door a piece of my mind. As mad as I was before, it no longer mattered as I got a glimpse at the sight before me. Wearing a pair of red Nike basketball shorts and a wife beater, he was the epitome of sexy. I never knew how much I missed him until now, as all my rage and fury became a thing of the past.

The way the sunlight hit his eyes had my ass in a trance. His beard and hair were crisp and cut to perfection, but the fresh scratches that now decorated his arms had my eyebrows shoot up in bewilderment. On top of that, I couldn't ignore that he wasn't dressed to go out and handle business like usual at this time of day. That only made my mind wonder even more. It didn't matter how hot it was outside. I knew that Nitro never wore basketball shorts outside the house. He considered it to be unprofessional, even with his career of being a dope boy. That told me that he had no plans of leaving this morning, but now, all my mind could wonder was . . . why?

"Wassup?" he said casually. "What you doing here?"

"I wanted to see you," I answered. "I missed you. Where's Gloria? She normally answers the door when you can't. That *is* her job, *right?*" I asked sarcastically.

"I gave her the day off. Next time, call before dropping by."

"I've never had to do that before," I replied, folding my arms across my chest. "Why do I have to start now?"

"Things have changed."

"Exactly *what* has changed?" I questioned.

"Listen to the voicemails that you sent me, and you'll get yo' answer," he said as he tried to close the door in my face.

"I'm sorry about that, baby," I pleaded as I placed my hand on the door to stop it from closing. "I was just upset. You know how I feel about you, but I'm better now. Besides, I thought you said that all was forgiven."

"And it is, no doubt, but I'm not gonna pretend it didn't happen. So until then, we need to take shit slow."

"What does that mean?" I asked as I felt myself become angry. "Aren't you gonna invite me in?"

"I'm kind of in the middle of something," he replied, casually looking behind him.

As he said that, I saw that bitch Myleena as she pranced her ass down the hallway. I was no longer infatuated with Nitro or how good he looked right now as I saw her as she headed to the kitchen. My eyes traveled down her petite but curvy frame. I could have spit fire for how mad I was when I saw what she was wearing.

A pair of blue and white shorts that stopped just below her ass cheeks. Shorts that hugged her hips so tight that they looked as if they were painted on her body. Not to mention how *well* the shorts showcased her ass. They matched with a white spaghetti strap shirt that showed off her perky breasts. This bitch looked like she could have been the mascot for man-snatching. I could see that my man was the first on her list. Tears filled my eyes as I looked back from her to him.

"So, *that's* why you're not inviting me in?" I asked as I nodded in Myleena's direction. "Because you're tapping her foreign ass?"

"Myleena, shit," he said as he caught his mistake. "I mean, LaToya, you need to go."

"*Really,* Nitro?" I asked as I stepped away from him. "*That's* how you feel? After everything I've done for you? After all the years we've been together?"

I was beyond hurt at him calling me that bitch's name. The same bitch who I once saw as no competition has now stolen my man from up under me. She has stolen my money, meal ticket, and life of the rich and glamorous that I felt was owed to me. The life that I thought I deserved. I couldn't describe the level of hurt, humiliation, and betrayal that I felt right now as I looked him in his eyes. I had done so much for him, and *this* is how he chose to repay me? But as clear as day, I could see his feelings toward me had changed. I was no longer his number one.

"*This* is how you do me, Nitro?" I asked again. "How could you do this to me?" I cried.

"Let's be real right now, LaToya," he said as he stepped outside. "You never loved me. Hell, I don't even know if you even liked me. Your only reason for being with me was for the money. Initially, that was cool because we both got what we wanted, but now, I want more."

"I can give you more," I cried. "I can give you so much more."

"I don't see you in that light, LaToya. I'm sorry."

I felt my heart shatter as he walked back into the house and closed the door. My thoughts raced as I walked back to my car and got in. I couldn't stop the tears from falling as I started my car and drove down the narrow road. In the back of my mind, I knew that I wasn't hurt because of love. In the back of my mind, I knew that I didn't love Nitro. I could never love anyone. Being hurt by people so much in the past made me build up a wall that prevented anyone or anything from getting too close to my heart . . . anything and anyone except for money. I knew that the dead presidents that decorated those dollars could never hurt me, but not having those dead presidents at the tip of my manicured fingertips could, in fact, kill me.

I cried as I picked up my phone and pressed the button to dial the last person I spoke to.

"Come on, Myleena! Fuck!" I screamed as I banged on my steering wheel and threw my phone down to the floor. "Damn you, Nitro!" I cried. "You even got me calling myself that bitch's name!"

I pulled over to the side of the road as I tried to gather myself. I was losing it and didn't know how to stop it. I took deep breaths as I looked down and picked up my phone.

"Hello," the voice on the other end of the receiver said.

"Hey. It's LaToya. I'm in," I cried as I broke down. "I want that nigga dead."

"Good choice," he said. I could hear the smile in his voice as he told me more about his plan. "In due time, that nigga Nitro will be six feet deep, and you'll rule as *my* queen."

"What about B?" I questioned. "I thought she was gonna be your queen?"

"That bitch is about to be a thing of the past. I'ma put two slugs in her ass as soon as I get what I want. She a bad bitch, but I need a smart bitch who's willing to do anything to make it to the top. I need a bitch like you."

I smiled wickedly at the thought of the streets knowing me and hailing me as their queen. It didn't matter that I didn't rule them. Truth be told, I never wanted to. I just wanted the benefits that came with it.

"Thanks, Beast. Just let me know what you need," I said before disconnecting the call.

I smiled as I got back on the road. If Nitro thought that he was just gonna leave me for that bitch, he had another think coming.

"Since you wanna be with that bitch, you can die with her."

Chapter Thirty-one

Nitro

(Three Weeks Later)

I sat back as my boys enjoyed the little kickback I had prepared for them. With so much stuff going on in the streets and with a war brewing with some new niggas, I felt like a party was exactly what they needed to take off the edge. My niggas worked so hard making that money, so I was sure to throw them a little get-together every once in a while to show my appreciation for their hard work.

With a shot of Patrón in my hand, I turned the television to the sports channel as I sat back and thought of future moves. As the official king of this empire, it was always my job to stay ten steps ahead of the rest, just as I saw my father do in the past. Any sign of weakness or lack of leadership would cause panic, which would surely cause anarchy. Anarchy within my kingdom would definitely result in niggas receiving two shots to the chest and one to the dome.

We were all brought together because of our love for one thing: money. So, at the end of the day, getting paid was always the motive, and getting richer was always the goal.

The room was filled with food, drinks, and women of different shades and ethnicities to keep their attention. My niggas were having the times of their lives as they laid hands on the women that pranced around the room in little to no clothing. My place was better than any strip club in the city as the women danced and touched on one another to get the attention of the men. As they touched each other, I listened to my niggas as they called dibs on which woman they were taking home for the night.

I, on the other hand, wasn't interested in any of it. My mind was on Myleena and how I felt myself falling increasingly in love with her every day. Although things didn't end well with LaToya and me, I knew it was time to cut it off before things got more complicated. Even with me calling it quits with LaToya, that didn't stop the numerous calls and text messages to my phone at all hours of the day and night. Myleena didn't voice anything, but I knew that it was starting to get to her.

"So, is there any word on who them niggas was that's responsible for the shootout at my mom's party?" I asked Ace as he sat next to me.

"Nah. Nothing has been confirmed," he replied. "But I put one of my girls on a nigga that's rumored to have had something to do with it or at least knows the person who was behind the shit."

"Okay," I replied as I nodded my head. "What about the niggas who shot my pops?"

"Yeah. I got Doc keeping tabs on him. Just waiting on yo' word."

"Bet."

Although the television was on, I wasn't paying any attention to it as Kevin Gates blasted through the speakers. I downed my shot before placing the glass on the table before me. Out of the corner of my eye, I looked at Ace as he stared at his phone before smiling. One thing about my boy Ace . . . He rarely smiled.

Looking at the clock, I saw that it was time for me to call this small meeting to order. Standing up, I looked down at Ace just as he looked at me.

"Time," I said as I walked to the center of the room.

"A'ight, everybody, time to get this meeting underway," I announced. "Ladies, if you'd be so kind as to wait in the next room."

They stood up from where they were and walked to the door that led to another sitting room. A few of the ladies winked at me as they brushed up against me on their way out, but like I said, I wasn't interested. Right now, Myleena was the only woman who had my eye.

"Take a seat," I instructed the rest of the fellas as I closed the door behind me.

I picked up my Chrome .22 from the side table and placed it on my waist as I walked over to the bar and poured myself another drink. Ace kept his eyes on the men as they sat at the big cherry wood conference table.

"A'ight, fellas. Y'all know why we here," Ace stated as I took my seat at the head of the table. "I'm sure y'all was enjoying yourselves, so I'll make this quick. I'm sure y'all all heard about the new niggas that's trying to move in on our turf."

"Man, fuck them niggas," Rico shouted as the rest joined in on a laugh. "*We* run this town!"

"Be smart . . . not cocky," I stated to Rico as I downed my drink. "Never underestimate a hungry nigga. They'll kill they own momma for a chance at the crown."

They all got quiet as they looked around the room at one another. It was rare that I spoke at these meetings. I always relayed my word to Ace, and he would give word to the rest. I looked at Rico as he calmed himself, and we all got back to the reason for the meeting.

"Now, your orders are to keep the block as cool as possible. But don't get me wrong. If them niggas step incorrect, you have permission to handle it, but I warn you to be as discreet as possible. One fuckup and the block gets hot, there goes our way of making money. Understand?"

"Understood," they all said in unison.

"Now, unless Nitro has anything else to add, the meeting is over."

Just as those words left his mouth, a door opened, but it wasn't the door that led to the other sitting room. It was the door that led to the rest of the house. Everyone's eyes looked over toward the door as Myleena walked in. Wearing a thin pair of red shorts and a matching crop top, she walked over to one of the end tables near the corner and grabbed her schoolbook.

My eyes were on her as she walked back across the room to the door. Her ass as it jiggled under the thin fabric of the sorts. Out of the corner of my eye, I saw Rico as he damn near broke his neck, trying to keep her in his view. My blood boiled as he practically drooled at the sight of her. I couldn't help the twitching of my eye as Rico stared at the door moments after she had left before he turned his attention back to us.

Ace shook his head as he sat at the other head of the table before looking from Rico to me.

"Damn, Nitro," Rico said as he shook his head in amazement. "I don't see how you do it. Ain't no way in hell I could be in a house with her ass and not hit that," he joked. "She definitely badder than LaToya's ass was."

"Is that right?" I asked sarcastically.

"You must be blind not to see all that ass."

"But yo' ass about to be," Mark said to Rico under his breath as he saw me grab my gun.

Now he noticed that my gun was now aimed at him. The color drained from his face, and fear set in his eyes.

"So, that's what you like?" I asked rhetorically as I got up and walked near him.

"Nah, man," he replied as he shook his head. "Nah."

"Nah, that's what you like," I confirmed. "If that's what you like, be a man about it and say that shit. I'm a man, and I can say that I like that. I'm a man who can say that ass is mine," I taunted. "But I'm also a man who's willing to die for it too. Are you?" I asked as I placed the gun on his left temple.

"Nah, man, I ain't."

"You should've thought about that at first."

I didn't even flinch as blood and brains spewed out the next second, and his body hit the floor. I looked around the room at all the niggas as they looked at Rico before shaking their heads.

"A nigga is going to be a nigga at the end of the day," my voice boomed as I looked around the room. "One thing I won't tolerate is disrespect. Understand?"

I didn't even wait for them to answer as I walked out of the room and slammed the door behind me. Them niggas should have known not ever to disrespect me. Now, it's time for me to explain that to Myleena.

Chapter Thirty-two

Myleena

I danced around my room as Beyoncé played in the background. I sang along with her as she sang about her man having a big ego. As I sang these words, I thought about Nitro and how happy he made me. I was on cloud nine as I thought about how he touched me. It's been three weeks since I gave him my virginity, and we've been making love every night ever since, even a few times throughout the day. I smiled as I thought of how passionate he was. So passionate that a chill ran down my spine just from thinking about how he had kissed every inch of my body.

I could feel myself blush as I went to turn down the music. It was a Friday night, and I had homework to finish. Dylan and Dionne had just left. Dylan ran off to be with his man, who Dionne often referred to as his sugar daddy, while Dionne went home to wait for Ace. I was happy to hear that she had finally made her move on him and that he was taking the time to get to know her. Although I hadn't known Dionne long, I could see that she was a nice and genuine person. From what I learned about Ace, he deserved a person like her. I could only hope that they were a good fit for each other.

I was just about to start on my schoolwork when the doors to my bedroom burst open. My heart dropped as

I jumped back, suddenly having flashbacks of the night that my family was murdered. I could slowly breathe again when I saw Nitro standing in my doorway, but my heart once again dropped at his look, which clearly stated that he wasn't happy. I looked around my room and quickly thought about what I could have possibly done to make him like this as he rushed toward me and pinned me to the wall.

"Don't you ever bring yo' ass downstairs dressed like that again," he threatened through clenched teeth. "What the fuck were you thinking?"

"I didn't know," I stammered. "I left my books down there from when we were studying earlier."

"You should have told me or Mrs. Valdez to get them for you. A nigga just had to die because he was looking at you," he whispered harshly in my ear.

"I'm sorry," I cried as tears blinded me.

Fear overclouded my thoughts as I closed my eyes to avoid looking at him. I couldn't control the floodgates as tears streamed down my face. To say that I was scared right now would have been an understatement. I couldn't bring myself to open my eyes until I felt his lips as they kissed mine before traveling to my tear-streaked cheeks.

"I'm sorry, baby," he said as he kissed my tears. "I'm so sorry. I don't know what came over me. Just seeing them niggas look at you did something to me. You're mine."

I opened my eyes to look at him. I looked into the beautiful eyes that I had fallen in love with. I saw the passion in them, but just as I saw passion, I saw fury, which scared me.

"So, you're telling me to stay in my room when you have company?"

"Nah. You ain't gotta stay in your room. Just cover up some more. I don't want men to see what I've claimed as mines."

I stared at him as he stared back at me. That rage in his eyes soon turned into lust as his hands ran up and down my exposed thighs. My breathing got heavy as his hands which were once roaming my thighs, now caressed my butt. Moans escaped my lips as he roughly grabbed it before he gently massaged it. Wrapping my arms around his neck, I closed my eyes and sucked on his neck as I enjoyed the feeling of being in his arms.

He wrapped my legs around his waist, carried me over to my dresser, and placed me on top of it. His lips made love to my neck and chest as he slipped my shorts over my hips. He never missed a beat as he slid them down my legs, and they fell to the floor. I looked at him lustfully as he slid my lace panties to the side and slipped a finger into my honeypot before placing his fingers into his mouth.

"Hmm," I moaned as I threw my head back against the wall as he continued to dip his fingers in and out of me before he placed them around my hips.

My legs were tightly wrapped around his waist, and I could feel his rod as it poked against his jeans, begging to be released. Just like he taught me, I swiftly undid his belt and button. I had no more patience left to wait as I pulled him even closer to me. I loved his aggression as he ripped my panties from my waist and threw them to the floor. I gripped the edge of the dresser as he slowly inserted himself into me.

My mind was gone, and all I could see were stars as he slowly glided into me. The way the tip of his dick hit my G-spot repeatedly was doing something to me. I was at his mercy as he made love to my body, love so good that I probably would've agreed to do anything just to keep this feeling.

"I'd kill a nigga without blinking if he ever looks at you," he groaned as he continued to thrust in and out of me.

"So, unless you want more niggas to die, I suggest you cover up. Understand?"

"Yes," I cried out as I held him tightly and as my toes curled. At that moment, I could feel his dick as it began to throb inside of me. "Yes!"

"Good," he said as he grabbed both of my thighs and gently pulled me forward as half my body hung from the dresser.

I kept my grip on the dresser as he pounded into me harder and faster, harder than he ever had. His hard thrusts only intensified the feeling that I felt building up in my stomach. It was happening. I felt myself on the verge of exploding.

"Aah," I screamed as my body clenched before it started to shake.

His strokes slowed down as he stuck his tongue into my mouth. I moaned and gently sucked what was left of my juices from his tongue as I continued to match his thrusts. Within minutes, I felt him as he exploded inside of me. Past exhausted, I smiled as he held me firmly and carried me to the bed before placing me on it. I enjoyed the feeling of myself throbbing as I looked up at him while he dressed again before he walked into my bathroom. I heard the sound of running water before he returned to me.

"Go clean yourself up, and when you're done, come downstairs. I have dinner waiting," he instructed before leaving my bedroom.

Chapter Thirty-three

LaToya

"Here, Bruno!" I said as I shoved two rolls of money into his hand. "It's all I got."

"This ain't even half of what was promised to me," he slurred as he took another sip from the bottle of Burnett's vodka. "I need all my money to get away from here."

"Bruno, that's $10,000. That's more than enough to get started somewhere. I'll send more as I get it," I replied in a hushed tone as I looked around the partially empty bar.

I could have kicked myself in the ass for agreeing to meet him in this place again. It wasn't filled with nothing but drunks and crackheads waiting on their next fix. As much as I wanted to ignore Bruno's ass, he had my ass backed into a corner. I now no longer wanted to be with Nitro, and with the fact that I was about to be the queen to another king, I still valued my life. I knew that with Nitro not yet dead, he still had power in these streets. If word got out that I was the one to order the hit at his mother's party, he would spare no expense on making sure that my ass was never seen or heard from again. Also, as I already knew, I was in too deep to go back now.

"Hell naw," Bruno drunkenly shouted. "I need *all* my money. I got you what you wanted. I shot that bitch."

"But you didn't kill her," I yelled. "She survived that shit. So, as far as I see it, you only deserve half of your cut!"

"Don't fuck with me, LaToya," he threatened through narrow eyes. "I want my money—all of it."

"You don't fuck with me," I challenged back. "I gave you all that I have. Now, you can either take it and leave town, or you can stay here and wait for Nitro and his boys to find your ass. It wouldn't bother me not one bit if I were to see yo' ass on the nine o'clock news floating in a river somewhere because, the way I see it, you're already dead," I hissed.

I looked at him, waiting to see if he would call my bluff. I knew that I was the one who was calling the shots, but at the same time, Bruno knew too much, and if he weren't so drunk all the time, he would have realized that he held all the cards that decided if I lived or died.

"You know what?" he asked sarcastically as he downed what was left in his bottle. "I'm a dead man anyways, but the difference between me and you is . . . I'm Nino when it comes to this shit."

I couldn't help but roll my eyes at his ass. He was so fucking drunk that he wasn't making a lick of sense. I wished like hell that I would have never made the plan to take out Myleena or Valentina. At this moment, I wished I had waited until I met Beast. One thing I could tell about Beast was that he was a man who was all about action. If he said he would do something, he did it. I calmed down to prevent myself from speaking my true thoughts, but as I did so, I pushed my thoughts of Beast to the back of my mind and refocused my attention back to Bruno.

"What the fuck are you talking about?" I asked smartly. "Yo' ass ain't no damn Nino. You ain't even a G Money. You ain't no damn kingpin. Shit, if you asked me, you're more like a Pookie before he got himself clean," I laughed.

"Nah. I'm like Nino," he repeated. "Like you said, I'm already dead, but if I'm going down, I'm taking a lot of motherfuckers with me."

"Motherfuckers like who?" I challenged.

"Motherfuckers like *you*," he spat as he threw the empty bottle at the wall.

I jumped as it shattered upon impact. I quickly turned back to Bruno. His drunken eyes were now bloodshot. They made him look crazed, almost sadistic. In fact, he resembled a rabid animal ready to attack as he looked at me as if I were his next prey.

"With just a simple touch of a button, I could end your life."

"Yeah. Right," I spat back. "You're too drunk to do anything. You must really think I'm dumb," I chuckled. "Anytime we ever talked about this plan, I was sure never to have anyone around who could identify me as being the culprit. So, in my eyes, you have *nothing*," I said cockily.

"Yeah? You think I'm such a drunk but never stopped to realize that I use that shit as a ploy. Yeah, I drink, but never past my limit of knowing that any mistake could jeopardize my life. I don't trust no one—not even family."

"What are you trying to tell me?" I asked.

"What I'm trying to tell you is that you were so busy thinking you're smart and so busy thinking I'm nothing but a worthless drunk that you never even realized that anytime we spoke, my phone was always in my hand or facing you. I have everything recorded, starting from the first night we talked about this shit all the way up to right now," he said as he held up his phone and pressed play on a video.

And as clear as day, I could see and hear myself as we discussed the time and date of Nitro's mother's party and how much I was willing to pay to ensure my problems were dealt with. Why the fuck didn't I notice this shit was all that I could ask myself. I may not have been in front of a mirror, but if I were, I'm sure that all the makeup and color from my face would have been completely drained. As I stared at Bruno, I just knew that I was paler than Casper.

"Not so confident now, are you?" he asked as he got up from his chair. "Now, I'll give you three days to come up with the rest of my money."

"So, you're just gonna sign your life away? For a hundred thousand dollars?" I asked, as I now understood the severity of the situation.

"My mother is dead; my only child is dead too. A hundred thousand dollars is all I saw myself as being worth anyway. So, what else do I have to lose if I don't get my money?"

My heart pounded as Bruno walked out of the bar. I was beyond shocked at the video that he showed me of us discussing the shooting. My thoughts were racing a mile a minute as I tried to think of a way out of yet another deep hole I had dug for myself. My hand shook uncontrollably as I held my car keys and walked out of the bar to my car. I tried to keep my emotions and tears at bay as I listened to the phone ring.

"Hello," Beast said as the call connected.

"Hey, babe."

"Whatchu need?"

"I have a problem."

"What else is new?" he asked with sarcasm. "Who is it, and what you need done?"

"It's my cousin, Bruno," I answered. "He has too much information that could destroy all our plans of taking over. I need for this problem to go away."

"Understood. So, what yo want me to do?"

I took a deep breath as I thought of the order I was about to give. When it came down to it, Bruno was my cousin. Just as he was blood, he made it clear that being blood meant nothing to him when money was involved. I never thought about taking his life in the beginning, but at this moment, it was either my blood or his blood. At the end of the day, I was choosing me over everything. That statement alone helped me render my verdict.

"Kill him."

Chapter Thirty-four

Beast

"I gotta go," I said as I got up from the bed where I had been lying.

"And go where at this time of night?" Bone asked as he looked at me. "Was that B?" he asked.

"Nah. That was LaToya," I answered. "I gotta go and handle something real quick."

"Why are you even bothered with that skeezer? She ain't nothing but a bitch looking for a nigga to take care of her."

"That bitch is a key pawn in us taking over these streets. So, until I get what I want, I gotta keep that bitch around."

I grabbed my keys off the nightstand and tucked my gun into the back of my pants. I took one last look at Bone as he lay in bed. Never in a million years did I ever think that the same feelings that I once held for a woman I would also hold for a man, but Bone was that man for me. The same strength and dominance that I had inflicted on women, I now had him inflict on me. Nah, I wasn't into men because of a family member touching me or a bad stay in prison. I've had this feeling resting inside me ever since I was a child, but back then, I was too scared to say it out loud. Now, I just didn't give a fuck.

The cool December air whipped past my face as I headed to my car. The sound of my phone pinging alerted me to a message. Seeing LaToya's name flash across the screen, I opened the message as an address was displayed. Wanting to get this over with, I quickly put the address into my GPS and followed it.

No more than twenty minutes later, I pulled up to a place that looked more like an abandoned crack house than it being a place where someone actually lived. I turned off my lights as there was a lot of foot traffic in and out of the house. People also sat on the front stoop. No sooner than I arrived than another message came in. It was a picture. I studied it as I looked at the house. I examined each face of the drunks on the porch until I matched one face with the image in the picture.

"There yo' ass is," I said as I placed a black bandanna on the bottom half of my face.

I may have been a hood nigga, but I was far from stupid. I was never foolish enough to have my face showing when I committed a crime, and I damn sure was never stupid enough to commit any crime with someone who could later be the reason I got caught. In this game, no one could be trusted. Not even the person you shared your bed with. They were all potential enemies, even when you reached the top.

Thoughts of being king raced through my mind as I exited my car and walked up to the house. LaToya was the key to that dream becoming a reality. Music was blaring as the people stumbled into each other and drunkenly danced with one another. My mark drank from a bottle and attempted to walk down the stairs.

"This is gonna be easier than I thought," I said to myself as he stumbled down the steps.

I reached behind me to check and make sure that my gun was still in place as the guy got closer to me. He looked like shit and reeked of liquor as he stumbled into me.

"My bad, homie," I said as he struggled to regain his balance.

"You better watch yo' motherfucking step," he shouted.

I smirked as he walked down the dark street that led to an alley. I took one last look at the people who stood on the porch to ensure no one was watching me. Just as I figured, their attention was all on one drunk woman as she stripped out of her clothing. I shook my head as I slowly walked toward my mark.

Even from a few feet away, I could hear him slurping from his bottle. He staggered over trash and broken bottles. I looked up at the flickering streetlights just as the man made a left into the alley. I heard cats screeching and smelled shit mixed with piss as I approached him.

Next, I heard the sound of piss hitting the brick wall, followed by the sound of his zipper being pulled up. I was inches away from him before he finally sensed my presence and turned around.

"Who sent you?" he asked as he used the wall to hold himself up.

"A friend," I answered with a wicked smile. I whipped out my gun and aimed it at his head.

Just as quick as I was with my gun, he was just as fast with his phone. I laughed as he held it to my head. This nigga must've been hella drunk as he held the phone in his hand as if it were a choppa.

"Whatchu gonna do with that?" I asked sarcastically. "Call 9-1-1?"

"Nah. Not at all. I already know who sent you," he said as he turned the phone to me. "LaToya will never reign these streets," he said as he pressed the send button. "Nitro will know everything very shortly," he snickered as he dropped the phone and smashed it with his feet.

Rage took over me as I emptied my clip into his head. His entire body jerked with each bullet that I pumped into him. The concrete ran red with his blood and splattered brains as I picked up the cracked phone.

"Fuck!" I cursed as I threw the broken phone at the wall. "Who the fuck did you send it to?" I asked as I repeatedly kicked his body.

"What's going on down there?" I heard someone ask above me.

I quickly looked up and wasted no time as I ran out of the alley and back to my car. "Fuck" was all that I could say as I peeled rubber down the block. Many thoughts crossed my mind about what had just happened. Here I was, thinking that the nigga was just a drunk. Come to find out, he was on to me from the very beginning.

"What the fuck did I get myself into?" I asked myself just as my phone began to ring.

Looking down, I once again saw LaToya's number. Although I wasn't in the mood to talk to her, I had to. I had to tell her what had just happened and that if that video got into the wrong hands, my life would be on the line. I knew that LaToya's loyalty was thinner than Tyra Banks's edges and knew that she would give up my ass if it meant that hers would be spared.

"Hello."

"Hey, baby," she sang. "Did you handle that problem of mines?"

"Yeah, I handled it."

"Good. Now come over here so I can give you your sticky treat," she purred.

"Yo' problem with ole' boy is solved, but whatever was on that video has been sent out. So, you might have a whole new problem on your hands."

"What do you mean, 'I'? You mean, 'we'?"

"Nah. You," I confirmed. "You too much of a liability. I can't handle the pressure right now."

"What am I supposed to do?" she yelled. "You're supposed to protect me. I'm supposed to be your queen. What am I going to do?"

I could hear the panic in her voice the more she spoke, but at the end of the day, this was the game she decided to play. It was time that she learned she had to play the hand she was dealt.

"I don't know what you gonna do. My only suggestion is that you get strapped and arm yourself with a bulletproof vest, because if this nigga is as dangerous and deadly as you say, you gonna need it," I told her as I disconnected the call.

Chapter Thirty-five

LaToya

(Two Days Later)

I cried and paced the floor as I continuously tried to dial Beast's number. It'd been two days since I got his call telling me that Bruno's last act on earth was sending out his video. I couldn't think of who he would send it to. As he said, he wasn't as dumb as I thought he was. He had a plan if things went sour, and they definitely had.

Still pacing, all I could ask myself was how I allowed my jealousy and quest for a lavish life to lead me down the path that was overshadowed by death. I couldn't figure out what went wrong. What was I going to do? Where was I going to go? I felt helpless.

"Damn it, Bruno," I cursed. "I hope you rot in hell."

I hated him for sealing my fate right along with his. I hated the fact that he was still able to ruin my life, even in death. My nerves were getting the best of me as my eyes darted back and forth to the door, and if truth be told, I was losing it. This used to be the one place where I truly felt safe. Unfortunately, after my phone call with Beast, I jumped at each and every bump that happened on the other side of the walls.

"Aah," I screamed as someone suddenly knocked at my door.

I slowly walked toward the door and grabbed a bat from a corner in the hall. My heart felt like it was about to jump out of my throat at the constant knocking. I took deep breaths and quietly slid the locks back and swung open the door, prepared to hit whoever was on the other side. The bat whipped through the air as it connected to the other side of the wall.

"What the fuck?" my girlfriend screamed as both of her arms flew up in the air. "What the fuck is going on?"

"What the hell are you doing here?" I yelled with the bat still in my hands.

"I was coming over to see if yo' ass wanted to go to a party with me, but it looks like yo' ass wanna go to the majors instead," she joked as she slowly walked through the door. "What's going on?"

"Nothing."

I was growing more paranoid by the second as I peeked my head out the door. I knew it was only a matter of time before Nitro got wind that my cousin was behind the entire thing and came looking for me. I had to think of somewhere to go until all this shit died down. After closing the door behind me and sliding the locks back, I placed the bat behind the door again.

"Now, bitch, care to tell me why you met me at the door with a bat?" she asked smartly with her hands on her hips.

"It's nothing," I lied. "With so much shit going on right now, I gotta be careful."

"Well, I came over to see how you were feeling. I know that you probably heard about what happened to Bruno. So, I figured you'd want a way to take your mind off it."

My heart dropped at the mention of Bruno. His face has been all over the news for the past two nights. Reporters questioned why a once most sought-after football player ended up with six shots in his head. Luckily, the police had no leads.

"Hello? LaToya, are you there?" she asked as she waved her hand back and forth in front of my face.

"I'm here," I replied, coming out of my daze.

"So, you up for a party?"

"Nah. Not tonight. I got some shit to figure out."

"Well, from the looks of things, shit's about to get real hot around here," she said as she got up from the couch and went to the door.

"What you mean?"

"You'll find out soon enough," she answered. "The streets are talking. Word is, yo' boo Nitro is still looking for whoever was behind the shooting at his mom's party. The streets say that there's gonna be a bloodbath."

"Is that right?"

"Yeah. So, be sure to stay safe. The last thing I need is to have to attend *your* funeral."

My eyebrows shot up at her last comment. Call me paranoid, but the way she talked to me led me to believe she knew more than what she was letting on. After she left, I quickly packed up my things. It was time to get out of Dodge.

Just as I stepped a foot out of my door, I was met with two gun barrels to my face.

"Get yo' ass back in the house, or I'll blow yo' head smooth off!"

Chapter Thirty-six

Unknown

"So, you think you would just fuck my nigga, and nothing would happen to you?" I said as I kept both the barrels of my gun to her head.

I kept my eyes on her as Courtney checked out the rest of the place to ensure no one else was around.

"Clear," Courtney said as she reemerged from the back and sat at the kitchen table.

"I don't know what you're talking about," LaToya stammered as she stumbled around.

"Beast, bitch! You fucking him, right?" I asked. "And just know my fingers get real trembly when I'm lied to."

"Yes, I have."

"Good girl," I coached. "It's good to see that you're a good listener. I just wished that you were better at picking the winning team."

"I'm not. Beast abandoned me," she cried. "He promised to make me his queen when he took the throne."

"Is that right?" I asked as I put down one of my guns. "Do you even *know* who I am?"

"No."

"So, you look to a man who fucks other men for protection?"

"What?"

I laughed as I used my free hand to retrieve my phone from my pocket. I was more than amused as her mouth dropped to the floor at the sight of Beast getting his ass pounded by another man.

"So, are you ready to be a part of a *winning* team now?"

"Yes," I said, as the thought of what I witnessed almost made me sick.

"Good. Take a seat and tell me everything you know," I instructed.

I knew the payoff would be well worth my loyalty, so I shared my information.

In just twenty minutes, I knew every plan that Beast had. Not to mention, I now knew of his plan to kill me as well as Courtney once he had everything that he needed to take over the streets. All this time, I was sending niggas out to find the missing piece to this puzzle when, all along, all I had to do was wait and be patient, and the piece soon came to me.

"Well, look at that," I said sarcastically. "You're cute *and* smart."

"I just want to live. After what I did, I need protection. Can you give me that?"

"Of course. Once you're down with me, you'll always be protected. I'll send a car to sit outside your place at all times. They'll be here if they get wind of something about to go down."

"Thank you so much."

"Now, I have to get going. I need to come up with a plan to get this fat bastard before he gets me."

"Wait," she said as we headed for the door, "I don't even know your name."

"Nabila."

Courtney trailed behind me as we walked back to my car.

"So, are you really gonna send some niggas to protect her?"

"Hell nah. That bitch is a snitch *and* a rat. I can't have that shit around me. The way I see it is, that bitch already dug her grave. So pretty soon, it's gonna be time for her to fill it."

Chapter Thirty-seven

Myleena

Two Days Later

I laughed with Dionne and Dylan as we walked through the mall. It was Saturday, the day of Ace and Dionne's first official date. I was so excited for her as we walked through the stores, looking for the perfect outfit for her.

"I missed y'all," Dylan pouted as we waited for Dionne to walk out of the dressing room.

"I missed you too," I replied with a smile.

"So, how has life been since the ugly step-mistress LaToya went *vamos*?"

"It's been great. Nitro and I have been—" I started before I stopped. I took a deep breath as I swallowed hard. I felt my face run hot, and my stomach got queasy as I looked at Dylan.

"Is you good?" he asked with perfectly arched eyebrows.

"Yeah, I'm good," I replied as I shook off the feeling.

Just as I opened my mouth to speak, the curtains to the dressing room opened, and Dionne strutted out. I was beyond amazed at how well the dress hugged her curves.

"What y'all think?" she asked. "You think Ace will like it?"

"You look beautiful," I replied. "Ace will *love* it."

"Shit, if he don't, he must be gay," Dylan said as he stood up to admire Dionne.

After pairing her dress with shoes and a few accessories, we were out the door and on our way to the food court. We laughed and joked about how the semester was nearly over and how we were ready to take our final exams.

"Y'all hungry?" Dylan asked as he looked at us.

"I could eat," I replied with a shrug.

"Me too," Dionne said.

"Cool. I got a taste for a burger," he said as he led the way over to Marco's Burgers.

I continued to laugh with Dionne as Dylan ordered his food. Then I looked at the burger as it cooked in the grease. Just the look and smell of it caused me to hurl over. Dionne and Dylan jumped back as I threw up everything I had eaten that morning. I was so embarrassed as people walked by and pointed at me.

"Don't worry, ma'am. I'll get that cleaned up," a worker said as he walked over with a mop and bucket.

"Thank you so much," I replied before rushing to the bathroom.

I looked at myself in the mirror as I rinsed my mouth. Thankfully, a vending machine that had gum was nearby. I closed my eyes as a wave of nausea subsided.

"What the hell was up with that?" Dionne asked as she burst through the doors, followed by Dylan.

"Hey!" a woman shouted at the sight of Dylan. "Women only!"

"Bitch, please. I look more feminine than you," he shot back as she angrily marched out the door. "Now, like Dionne said, what was up with that?"

"I don't know," I said as I shook my head and wiped my mouth again. "I must have eaten something bad. As soon as I smelled them burgers, I got sick. I couldn't help myself."

I looked at them through the mirror as they looked at each other. It was as if they were talking with their eyes as they turned back to face me.

"You said that you lost your virginity about two months ago, right?" Dylan asked.

"Yes."

"Were y'all using condoms?" Dionne inquired.

"It wasn't planned."

"When was your last period?"

"A few months ago," I answered. "But my periods were never regular."

"Well, only one way to find out for sure," they both said as they grabbed me by the arm and dragged me out of the mall.

I bit my nails down to the nubs as Dylan drove recklessly through the city until we came to CVS. It wasn't his driving that had me nervous. It was the thought of being pregnant and forever shaming my family for being pregnant by a man that I wasn't married to. We weren't even in a relationship. I waited in the backseat as Dionne and Dylan walked into the store. My thoughts were killing me to the point that I couldn't find the strength to get out of the car as so many possibilities floated through my head.

"Got it," Dionne announced as she and Dylan jumped back into the car.

It seemed like time flew by as we arrived back at the house. I sat on the toilet with the test between my legs. I was sitting on pins and needles as the hourglass on the test tipped from one side to the other.

"Am I gonna be a sexy auntie or what?" Dylan asked, breaking the silence.

I could have fainted at the thought of being a single mother. It just wasn't our custom, and the few women who did have children out of wedlock had horrible reputations and were treated even worse.

"The results are in . . ." Dionne announced as she held the test in her hand.

As if this moment couldn't get any worse, just as she said those words, Nitro walked in. Upon entering the room, he looked from me to Dionne and Dylan.

"What's going on?" he asked.

"Looks like you're gonna be a daddy," Dylan announced with a smile. "Positive," he said, showing me the test.

The room felt as if it were spinning, and my legs felt like jelly as I collapsed to the floor. I woke up to Nitro standing over me as I rose from my bed.

"What happened?" I asked as I looked for Dionne and Dylan.

"You fainted," he answered.

My chest heaved up and down as my anxiety rose. I looked at Nitro as I tried to gather my thoughts, but the image of a positive pregnancy sign was all that I could see.

"Pregnant?" I asked, still in shock.

"Yeah. Pregnant," he repeated. "So, what do you want to do about this?"

I looked at him as if he had somehow sprouted a second head.

"What do you mean, 'me'? Don't you mean 'we'?"

"Myleena, I'm cool with it either way. I wasn't ready for children, but I knew what we were doing and knew that there was a chance of you getting pregnant."

"I can't be pregnant!" I shouted as I jumped up and began pacing. "This is the exact reason why my father disowned my sister! What am I going to do?" I cried. "I'm not married."

When I looked at Nitro, I could feel myself growing upset at how nonchalant he was acting. This was my life that was hanging in the balance.

"We have to get married! My father would kill me!" I was going crazy at the thought of having a baby by myself.

This was considered to be the worst sin in our country. I had heard so many stories of women getting stoned to death and even having their heads cut off for having children out of wedlock. "We have to get married! I can't be a single mother! I just can't!" I repeated over and over. "What would my father say?"

"Yo' father ain't saying shit! Yo' father is dead!" Nitro shouted back at me.

"This isn't traditional. I can't do this," I said, dropping to the floor.

"You once told me that you envied the American way, right?" he asked as he looked down at me. "Well, this is it. Congratulations. I'll be with you every step of the way if you decide to keep the baby or get rid of it, but I'm not ready for marriage," he stated as he walked out the door and left me to my thoughts.

My thoughts were in a whirlwind as I tried to see how I allowed my life to spiral out of control.

"I can't do this," I repeated as I got up from the floor.

I walked over to the mirror and stared at my reflection. I cried at the person who stared back at me. As I looked at myself, I no longer saw myself. I saw my sister. As I looked down, I saw myself with a pregnant belly but with no husband. It's the opposite of the way it's supposed to be. I couldn't do it. I couldn't ruin my life like that . . . not if I could help it.

Picking up my phone, I dialed the only person who was by my side throughout everything. I sniffled back the tears as the phone rang.

"Valentina," she said once the calls connected.

"Hey, Mrs. Valentina."

"How are you, honey?"

"Not good," I cried.

"What's wrong?"

"I love your son, but I don't know if he feels the same. I got myself in trouble."

"What kind of trouble?" she asked.

"I just can't be here anymore. Is there anywhere else that I can stay? I can't be around him right now," I said as I broke down on the phone.

"Don't cry, baby girl. We have several places where you can go. Give me about an hour, and I'll have everything situated," she said before ending the call.

Chapter Thirty-eight

Nitro

I thought of Myleena and thoughts of being a father as I drove down the street. Although deep down in my heart, I knew that I loved her and wanted to be with her, at the same time, I wasn't sure if I could to commit to forever, a marriage. To some, it might not have been that big of a deal, but I wanted to be sure that the person I married was the person I was supposed to be with.

"Damn," was all that I could say as I rode over to Ace's place. "Pregnant."

The more I thought of Myleena being pregnant, the more I wondered if I was ready to commit to being someone's father. Sure, I had more money than I knew what to do with, but coming from money, I knew it wasn't all that a kid needed to be happy. Not just money, with me being in the game, I wondered if I'd even be around long enough to show him what my father showed me.

The sound of Ace climbing in the front seat and slamming the door behind him distracted me. I shook my head as I sparked a blunt that sat in the ashtray.

"What's going on?" I asked as I pulled from the curb.

"Not a damn thing. Just got word from Bear that he had to clip one of them new niggas," he informed me. "But don't worry. He followed orders and was discreet about it."

I was too much into my thoughts to comprehend what Ace was saying. I just couldn't help but think of my last words to Myleena. I knew that I must have sounded cruel and uncaring, but at the end of the day, I wasn't the type of nigga who could be pressured into doing anything.

"Dude, what the hell is going on with you?" Ace asked as we approached a red light. "Yo' mind ain't here."

"Myleena," I answered as I saw a cloud of smoke from the corner of my eye. "She's pregnant."

"Say what? How the fuck? When the fuck?"

I could only shake my head as he rattled off question after question. As he asked questions, I pulled over to the side of the road. I couldn't think anymore as I stepped out and walked over to the woman who stood in front of the smoking car. Some would think that I was just being a Good Samaritan, but truth be told, I was running away from the questions that Ace was asking, running away from myself for not knowing the answers to his questions.

"Hey, you need some help?" I asked.

Turning around, I laid eyes on a beautiful pair of honey-brown eyes. I looked at the sweat dripping from her forehead and nose. As I looked at her closer, I realized it was the same chick I ran into the night at the club.

"Small world," I chuckled.

"Very," she agreed.

"Do you need some help?" I asked again after looking down at her smoking hood.

"Actually, I do," she chuckled. "You know anything about cars?"

"I know a little something. You got a rag?"

I got a good glimpse of her slim waist and thick ass as she walked to the passenger side. A small smile graced her face as she looked over her shoulder and found me staring. Seconds later, she passed me a thick black shirt that I used to fan away the smoke. After a few minutes of checking, I found the problem.

"So, when was the last time you got oil?"

"Oh, don't make me lie to you," she chuckled. "I usually wait until I see lights on the dash."

"Well, I'd suggest that you never do that again."

"So, what's wrong with my car?"

"Looks like due to no oil, your engine has locked, and from my understanding of cars, that's probably more than what this car is worth."

"So, basically, what you're telling me is that my car is junk."

"Pretty much," I answered. "Would you like a ride to wherever you were heading?"

"Umm, no. I don't know how my boyfriend would react to that, but could I use your phone to call a tow truck and maybe an Uber?"

"So, you do have a man?" I asked slyly.

Instead of responding, she just smiled as she continued to look at me. I kept my eyes on her as she made her phone call. The way the sun hit her eyes perfectly was mesmerizing. Although I found it odd that she didn't have a phone, I shrugged it off and allowed her to use mine.

Thoughts of Myleena and the baby crossed my mind as I looked at the sunny sky. I felt shame for how I spoke to her before leaving the house. I knew my words may have sounded cruel, but I needed her to understand that she was no longer in her country. She was in America, and having a child out of wedlock wasn't a death sentence here.

"Hey," the girl said, pulling me away from my thoughts. "I'm done. Thank you so much."

"No problem at all. Did they say how long of a wait you had?"

"They said about twenty minutes."

"Well, I guess I could sit with you as you wait."

"Oh no," she said as she shook her head. "I couldn't ask you to do that."

"You didn't ask," I corrected. "I offered."

She instantly blushed as she agreed to me waiting with her. We both sat on the hood of her car and talked. As she spoke and told me about herself, I could hear a slight accent in her speech, but it was often covered up with a slight hood accent.

"So, where are you from?" I found myself asking. "From your accent, I can tell you're not American."

"I'm not. I'm from a place far away from here. A place that I never want to go back to."

"And family?"

"No. My entire family is dead."

"Oh. I'm so sorry to hear that."

"Don't be. Even before they died, they washed their hands of me," she replied. "So, it was easy to mourn their deaths."

"Why did they wash their hands of you?" I found myself wanting to know.

"Because I chose to live my life differently from the way they lived theirs."

"I can respect that," I agreed.

Seconds later, her Uber was pulling up. She thanked me as she got in the backseat of the car.

"What's your name?" I called out as she began to roll up her window.

"It's Nabila."

I couldn't ignore how attractive she was as I walked back to my car and jumped into the driver's seat. I had utterly forgotten that Ace was even in the car.

"It's about damn time," Ace said as I pulled from the curb. "I thought I was gonna have to send a search party after yo' ass."

"Whatever, nigga."

"Well, why yo' ass was playing Captain Save A Ho, I finally got a good lead on the shooters from yo' momma's party."

"Is that right? Who is it?"

"Some nigga name Bruno, but the crazy thing about that is, it's the same nigga that they found shot up in an alley a few days ago. I got Rock sending me a picture from that night. That way, we can put a face to the name. It turns out the nigga was closer to yo' mom's than we thought."

Just as soon as those words left his mouth, his phone pinged, alerting him that he had a message. Not even seconds after Ace's phone pinged, my phone started ringing. I saw my mother's name flash across my screen.

"Wassup, Ma?" I asked once the calls connected.

"What the fuck is going on?" she yelled. "What did you do to Myleena?"

"What are you talking about?"

"Fuck what I'm talking about. What I wanna know is what did *you* do to Myleena. Why is she calling me telling me that she needs to move out? What the fuck is going on over there?"

"She's pregnant."

"Pregnant? How the fuck did that happen? By who?"

"By me."

"I'm gonna kick yo' ass, Nitro. You know better."

"Ma, I really ain't got time for this shit. I got other things to tend to."

"What yo' mouth when you talk to me. Speaking of things to tend to, you might wanna make yo' way up here."

"Why?"

"Yo' father is up," she announced.

It felt like a huge weight was lifted from my shoulders, weight that I didn't even know I was still holding on to. I made a U-turn in the middle of the street as I headed in the opposite direction toward the hospital. I raced like a bat out of hell to the hospital and barely put the car in park before Ace and I jumped out and were on the elevator.

"Aye, I got that picture," Ace said as he handed me the phone.

My blood was boiling, and I could feel my jaws flexing as I looked at the picture of the person responsible for the shooting at my mother's party.

"You know who that is?"

"Yeah. That's Bruno," I answered. "LaToya's cousin."

The elevator dinged, signaling that we had reached our floor, but instead of getting off, I stayed on. As much as I wanted to see my father and let him know everything was good, I couldn't. I had a loose end to tie up before saying those words: "That bitch is dead!"

To Be Continued . . .